Anna Abney is among the last descendants of the Abney family, former residents of Measham Hall, a lost house of Derbyshire. She taught English and Creative Writing at the Open University and wrote her PhD on the seventeenth-century writer Margaret Cavendish. She lives in Kent with her husband.

Praise for the Measham Hall series

'It's rare for a historical novel to feel so timely'
Jo Baker, *Sunday Times*-bestselling author of *Longbourn*

'Political subterfuge and family secrets entwine in this tale of historical intrigue, set during the late seventeenth-century tensions between Protestants and Catholics. Meticulously researched and alive with intricate period details to savour, I raced through it, while learning huge amounts' Lucy Ribchester, author of *The Amber Shadows*

'Impeccably researched and wonderfully atmospheric, with a heroine you can't help rooting for' Frances Quinn, author of *The Smallest Man*

'Exciting and immersive. It took me straight into the heart of Restoration England in all its rich and vivid detail. I was gripped!'
Nicola Cornick, author of *House of Shadows*

'In elegant prose, this enthralling novel puts a human face to the trials, terrors and enduring hopes of the plague years'
Catherine Meyrick, author of *The Bridled Tongue*

'By turns humorous and heart-wrenching, impeccably researched and beautifully written throughout, this is a haunting and original debut that demands to be read'
Lianne Dillsworth, author of *Theatre of Marvels*

Also by Anna Abney

The
SECRET
CHRISTMAS

ANNA ABNEY

DUCKWORTH

First published in the United Kingdom by Duckworth,
an imprint of Duckworth Books Ltd, in 2024

Duckworth, an imprint of Duckworth Books Ltd
1 Golden Court, Richmond, TW9 1EU, United Kingdom
www.duckworthbooks.co.uk

For bulk and special sales please contact
info@duckworthbooks.com

A CIP catalogue record of this book is
available from the British Library

Typeset by Danny Lyle

Print and bound in Great Britain by CPI Ltd, Croydon, CR0 4YY

Hardback ISBN: 9780715655573

eISBN: 9780715655580

Characters

The Measham Hall household
Sir Nicholas Hawthorne
Lady Agnes Hawthorne
William Hawthorne – their son
Alethea Hawthorne – their daughter
Marion – waiting-woman and nurse, cousin of Agnes
Norris – servant
Tickell – the cook
Tom – kitchen-boy

John Thornly Senior – the bailiff
Mrs Thornly
Young John Thornly – their son

Mr Yeavlea – Puritan neighbour

Travelling players
Valentine Evans – leader of the troupe
Susanna Evans
Fortuna
Gregory Alleyn
Robert Hart
Michael Lowin
Abraham Palmes
Stephen Wallis

There were lately some over curious, hot zealous Brethren, who with a superbian predominance did doe what they could to keep Christmas day out of England; ... they were of opinions, that from the 24 of December at night, till the 7 of January following, that Plumb-Pottage was meer Popery, that a Coller of Brawn was an abomination, that Roast Beef was Antichristian, that Mince Pies were Reliques of the Whore of Babylon and a Goose, a Turkey, or a Capon, were marks of the Beast.

John Taylor, *Christmas in & out, or,*
Our Lord & Saviour Christs birth-day, 1652.

A BILL OF FARE FOR CHRISTMAS DAY

First Course
A Coller of Brawn with a large spring of Rosemary iced
Stewed broth of Mutton and Marrowbones
Boil'd Partridge
A Sur-loyn of Beef
Minced Pyes
A made dish of Sweet-breads
A roasted Swan
A Venison Pasty
A Steak Pye
Venison roasted
A Turkey stuck with Cloves and roasted
Bran Geese roasted
Roasted Capons
Custards

Second Course
A whole Kid roasted
Two couple of Rabbets, two larded
A Pig souc'd with Tongues
Three Ducks, one larded
Three Pheasants, one larded
A Swan Pye
Three brace of Partridges, one larded
Half a dozen Teal roasted
Half a dozen Plovers, some larded and roasted
A Quince-Pye
Half a dozen Wood-cocks, some larded
Two dozen Larks roasted
Powdered Geese
Sturgeon
Dryed Neats Tongues

(The Compleat Cook)

✣ Chapter One ✦

21st December 1653

To make good Minced Pies
Take one Pound and half of Veal parboiled, and as
much Sewet, shred them very fine, then put in 2 pounds
of Raisins, 2 pound Currans, 1 pound of Prunes, 6
Dates, some beaten Spice, a few Caroway seeds, a little
Salt, Verjuice, Rosewater and Sugar, so fill your Pies, and
let them stand one hour in the Oven: When they go to
Table strew on fine Sugar.

(Hannah Woolley, *The queen-like closet*)

A sharp December wind was buffeting the sides of the carriage, but Alethea sat comfortably nestled between her mother and her nurse, cushioned by their thickly padded bodies against the jolting of the wheels. She pitied William, who sat opposite, next to their father. Despite his cloak and the blanket their mother had tucked over him, William's face was pinched and pale. Alethea thought he was probably clenching his teeth and hoped he wasn't going to be sick like he had been when Grandfather took them to Preston in his coach. She did not think their father would be as amiable about it as Grandfather had been.

Now that Father had fallen asleep, Alethea was able to study his face. He looked more approachable in repose; the heavy lines that gave his brow a cross expression were smoothed out and his mouth, though still turned down at the corners, was at least not scowling. He looked closer to how she had pictured him in her head.

So much had been made of Sir Nicholas's return from banishment that she had been as excited as the rest of the family to see him again, though she was the only one who didn't remember him, being but two years of age when he had been forced to flee the country. She had imagined a man like Grandfather Ormerod, only younger and more handsome. One who would swing her in his arms and carry her on his shoulders, who would take her riding and tell her stories of his adventures beyond the seas. Certainly her mother had spoken of him as though he were a prince who was going to restore his family to their rightful castle.

The carriage jolted over something in the road and his eyes opened instantly, fastening on hers before she could look away. To her surprise he winked at her. She smiled and in response the corners of his mouth twitched upwards.

'All right, William?' he asked, turning to the boy beside him.

'Yes, thank you, sir,' William answered through gritted teeth.

Lifting the leather covering, Sir Nicholas peered out of the window. 'Shouldn't be too much further now, though it's hard to tell exactly where we are. That's one of the reasons I prefer to travel on horseback. Coaches are all very well for ladies, but a man needs his own horse, hey, William?' He nudged his son with his elbow.

Flinching, William managed to nod his head. His skin had a distinctly green tinge to it.

'Perhaps we could stop and take a little air,' their mother suggested. 'It must be several hours since we left the inn.'

'Do you need to alight for a moment?' Sir Nicholas asked her, his voice more tender.

'I would be grateful,' Lady Agnes said. 'And perhaps William could ride on one of the horses or up on the box? He'll get a better view of the country and see Measham as we approach.'

'We'll both ride up on top.' Sir Nicholas rapped on the roof of the coach with his fist.

They could hear the coachman calling to the horses and the coach jerked to a halt. Marion, Agnes's waiting-woman, who was now also the children's nurse, woke with a start.

'Are we under attack?' she cried.

'William needs to sit outside,' Alethea proffered. 'He is squeamish again.'

Her brother knocked Alethea's leg with his sword as he followed Father out of the coach. She was tempted to kick him, but restrained herself. Just as well the short sword was in its scabbard or it might have torn her skirt.

A gust of cold air blew in through the open door and Alethea lifted her face to it, savouring the freshness. She had to wait until everyone else had alighted before she could be released and she leapt impatiently from the steps, landing in a puddle, which caused Marion to cry out again, in anger this time.

Looking up at the silvery-brown branches arching over the road, Alethea caught sight of the fiery tail of a squirrel as it darted along a bough. Robins, blackbirds, finches and fieldfares were all singing from the hedgerows and in the ditches a stream babbled. The road curved ahead so invitingly, it seemed to call to her and she longed to ride on the outside too so that she could take in all the sights and sounds of the land as they travelled through it. She had been told so much about the splendour of Measham Hall and the bountiful pastures that surrounded it, she couldn't bear to be denied the views William was to enjoy.

'May I ride one of the horses, sir?' she asked her father. It was the first time she'd dared to address him directly, but his recent smile had encouraged her.

'We can't unharness the horses, but a little sparrow like you won't take up much room alongside your brother. If you don't mind their company, Fletcher?' Sir Nicholas looked up at the driver.

'With all due respect, sir, wouldn't it be safer to keep the children inside?' Marion came to stand beside them, pulling her hood up against the wind. 'They could catch a chill out here and what if the carriage turns over? They'll be thrown goodness knows where, their heads smashed open on rocks, or their bodies impaled on branches.' She gestured dramatically to the thickets of brambles growing at the side of the muddy road. 'Or, God forbid, if we're besieged by brigands, they could be shot at, or stolen from us.' Marion clasped her hands against her bosom.

Alethea glared at her. She suspected Marion would relish such an exciting encounter, especially if it did away with her charges. Grandmother Ormerod often chastised Marion for her fantastical imagination.

'I've seen boys not much older than William ride into battle.' Sir Nicholas was looking over at his son with a disappointed expression.

William was leaning, shivering, against a tree while Agnes wiped his face with a cloth.

'William has a delicate stomach, always has done,' Marion observed.

'The air will do him good, but you can take the little maid back inside with you.'

'Come along.' Marion began pushing Alethea towards the open door. 'Ladies don't want to be outside, tossed about by the weather.' When Alethea resisted, Marion patted her on the head. 'Someone who doesn't like to have their hair brushed should be careful not to get it tangled.'

Sir Nicholas was about to climb up onto the box beside the driver, when the earth beneath them began to tremble and the sound of approaching horses came thundering down the track. Agnes rushed over with William and the family stood in a tight knot by the side of the coach. Even Sir Nicholas's heart was beating wildly. Perhaps Marion's imagination wasn't so fantastical after all, or by mentioning brigands she had summoned them up, Alethea speculated.

The riders were soon close enough to be recognised as an armed militia. They drew up, three men on either side of the coach.

'Good morning,' their captain called in a friendly tone.

Chapter One

'Morning,' Sir Nicholas replied, though he thought by now it must be well past noon.

'Where are you good people travelling to?' the captain enquired.

'We are going home to Measham Hall,' Sir Nicholas explained, pulling his pass out of his pocket. Despite the captain's amicable manner, he knew what the next question would be.

Taking the pass, the captain studied it carefully. 'I see you are papists; you will know therefore that it is illegal for you to carry arms. My men will need to search you to ensure you are abiding by the law.' The captain sounded rather sorrowful, as if the whole process pained him, or perhaps it was the existence of Catholics that grieved him.

'I understand.' Sir Nicholas knew better than to provoke him. He didn't like to look at his son in case that drew the soldiers' attention to the boy. Would they believe him if he told them William's sword was just a toy? The blade was sharp enough for it to be used as a weapon. He cursed himself now for giving it to William; it had been a foolish gift. He hadn't considered the ban on arms when he'd brought it back from France. He'd been lucky it hadn't been found before now.

The soldiers proceeded to search Sir Nicholas and the driver, as well as the interior of the coach, before moving on to the baggage tied to the roof.

'Is that really necessary?' Sir Nicholas asked the captain. 'We have a long journey ahead of us and wish to reach our destination before nightfall. We would be grateful if you can allow us to continue on our way.' The very taste of the words in his mouth were nauseating to him. To think he was come to this, to bow and scrape to these upstarts.

'We have to be thorough.' The captain scrutinised the faces of each of the family in turn. 'We are seeking a young man suspected of treason against the Commonwealth. He is believed to be carrying correspondence to Charles Stuart, son of the late tyrant. Anyone who assists this enemy of Parliament will likewise be considered a traitor and will be imprisoned and dealt with according to the law.' His voice was sterner now.

'I can assure you, we have had no dealings with anyone of that nature. I am a man of my word; I have sworn the oath of engagement and will not renege on my promise to be faithful to the Commonwealth of England.' Sir Nicholas placed one hand over his heart as if to prove his sincerity.

'The Commonwealth of England as it is now established, without a king or House of Lords,' the captain added with some emphasis. 'Met anyone on the road? Taken on any passengers?' Instead of addressing Sir Nicholas, he looked at William, as though the boy might be more likely to blurt out the truth than his father.

William, his dark eyes huge in his pale face, shook his head emphatically.

'Sir.' One of the soldiers looked at his captain and gestured to the women. 'Shall we search the ladies?'

Marion gazed up at the captain, her blue eyes wide with a mixture of fear and entreaty. Agnes kept her eyes fixed on her children; she had drawn them in close to her, clasping their hands in hers.

The captain shook his head. 'We are not brutes; we know how to treat women with respect.' He emphasised the 'we' as if to indicate their superiority over their royalist enemies.

When the militia finally departed, Sir Nicholas bent down beside William. 'Where's the short sword I gave you?'

'I have it,' Agnes said. She opened her cloak to reveal William's belt strapped round her waist, the sword and scabbard attached to it concealed in the folds of her skirt.

'That was well done.' Sir Nicholas regarded her with new admiration.

Agnes said nothing. She had tried to dissuade her husband from giving the sword to William but he had overruled her. They were fortunate the captain had been so chivalrous.

'Come on, William,' Sir Nicholas said with unconvincing jollity. 'We'll leave your smiter in the care of your mother while we ride up on top.' Grabbing William's arm, he hauled the boy up behind him onto the coach-box.

Chapter One

'Mother...' Alethea began.

'Get into the coach with Marion,' her mother answered curtly.

Alethea felt as though she were being stuffed into a chest. After her brief moment in the wintry sunlight, she was only too conscious of how dark and fetid it was inside the carriage. The air smelt of farts and sweat. She kicked her heels against the underside of the seat. William might be the son and heir, but he was unlikely to appreciate the view of Measham Hall as much as she would. He would be concentrating on keeping the contents of his stomach down, whereas she would have taken in everything. If only she could be riding on high, looking out at the trees and the fields and enjoying the vast expanse of white sky above, instead of cooped up in here with her mother and Marion.

'No need to be pettish,' Marion chided. 'We'll still be at Measham Hall before it's dark. Isn't that something to rejoice at?'

'You haven't even seen Measham Hall,' Alethea retorted.

'I've been told all about it,' Marion answered firmly.

Alethea scowled. She couldn't understand why Mother had chosen to bring Marion to act as both her own maid and their nurse. Marion was a distant cousin and there had been some talk among the adults about a broken betrothal. Alethea had not been allowed to hear the whole story, but there seemed to be something shameful about it. Perhaps the intended bridegroom had caught sight of Marion's crooked teeth, though she usually kept her thin lips pinched shut in order to hide them, Alethea thought uncharitably.

Agnes had resumed her seat beside them and the coach began to move again, bumping slowly over the rutted road.

'You were very brave to conceal the sword like that, My Lady,' Marion said. 'Quick-witted too. It's just as well you have such a dainty waist. But how did you get the belt on so swiftly?'

'William was in such discomfort he loosened the buckle and it fell onto the ground. When I heard the horses approach I put it on. I feared we might be stopped.' Agnes adjusted the scabbard beneath her cloak.

'May I wear it, Mother?' Alethea asked hopefully.

'A sword is not a plaything.' Sighing, Agnes lowered her eyelids for a moment.

'The captain was very handsome, for a Parliament-man,' Marion said musingly, coiling a butter-coloured curl around her finger.

Opening her eyes again, Agnes gave her cousin a disapproving look. 'I hope Norris arrived at Measham Hall in good time.' Norris was her parents' servant and had travelled on ahead with a wagonload of household goods. 'He said he would bring a boy to help and would make sure the fires are lit and the house warmed.' She pulled her cloak more tightly round her narrow shoulders. 'It's a shame I couldn't send a few maids down with him to clean the place. I wonder if Ann Beddingfield received my letter about hiring servants for me. I had hoped to hear from her before we left Owlcote.'

Agnes blinked rapidly and Alethea noticed for the first time the dark grey shadows beneath her mother's eyes. Agnes had been preoccupied for weeks with trying to find servants for Measham Hall. Alethea had overheard her say that very few were willing to work for a man branded a delinquent and a papist. She understood that her family were papists because they followed the old religion, but asked Grandfather Ormerod what a 'delinquent' was. He said they were men who had fought for His Majesty and were now being punished for their loyalty by the victorious Parliamentarians.

'We'll soon have the house fit for a king,' Marion was assuring Agnes. 'I can get down on my knees and scrub the floors myself if necessary.'

Alethea nearly snorted, for Marion had very fixed ideas about her position in the family, which certainly didn't include her being reduced to doing scullion-work.

'I wouldn't expect that of you.' Agnes gave Marion a weary smile. 'Mr Quires assured me the soldiers who were garrisoned at Measham were all godly men who had treated the property with respect.' She sighed. 'Sir Nicholas paid enough to get it back, they should at least return it to us in a habitable condition.'

'We know what we can expect from puritans.' Marion raised her eyebrows, then seeing Agnes's face cloud over, added quickly, 'Just think, you will soon be mistress of your own house again and can resume the position due to you.' She leant back in her seat and a dreamy expression came over her angular face. 'We shall have a splendid Christmas back at Measham Hall.'

Alethea closed her eyes and tried to picture her new home. Soon it began to resemble a castle, with towers, balconies and elaborate parapets. A moat with swans swimming in it encircled the walls and over an arched bridge lay beautiful gardens, with a maze, a bowling green and all manner of statues. There were tennis courts next to the stables and Father would buy her a horse of her own and take her hunting through the deer parks and woods. In the summer there would be peaches, apricots and strawberries. She could almost taste the sweet fruit and licked her lips in anticipation.

'Poor child, she must be thirsty,' Agnes said, seeing Alethea's mouth moving in her sleep.

The sun was already dropping behind the hills by the time they reached Measham Hall and far from appearing bright and welcoming, in the gloom of dusk the house looked dark and desolate. Only the smoke curling up from the chimneys gave any indication that it might be inhabited.

The Hawthornes disembarked once more, this time more slowly, and stood on the overgrown avenue, stretching out their cramped limbs. Sir Nicholas helped the driver to untie the cases from the roof of the coach.

'Well, at least we won't need to decorate the outside of the house,' Agnes said with forced cheer, looking up at the ivy-covered upper-storey windows. 'That task has been done for us.'

No one referred to the lower windows, which had been smashed and were covered with thin wooden boards.

'Why are you talking about decorations when you know full well Christmas is prohibited?' Sir Nicholas asked impatiently.

Alethea slipped her hand into her mother's and felt a reassuring squeeze from Agnes. 'We marked Christmas at Grandfather's,' Alethea whispered.

Unfortunately, her father overheard her. 'The man should have had more sense,' he said roughly.

Aleathea shrank back against her mother's skirts.

'Your grandparents weren't under the scrutiny that we are. If I put a step wrong there's those as would be only too happy to see me hang.' Sir Nicholas tried to speak more gently, but he wasn't accustomed to talking to children and in attempting to emphasise the gravity of their circumstances he sounded angrier than he had intended.

'Forgive me, sir,' Alethea mumbled.

William, having recovered from his earlier distemper, had run off into the gardens to explore and now he reappeared dragging a bough of holly, its dark green leaves laden with clusters of crimson berries.

'Look what I found,' he called jubilantly.

'And what are you planning on doing with that?' Sir Nicholas demanded.

All the joy fled from William's face. 'For the decorations?'

'Haven't you explained to these children that the Christmas holiday has been abolished by Parliament?' Sir Nicholas turned to William and Alethea, enunciating slowly, 'The churches must not open for Christmas services. Feasting, dancing, songs and games are all forbidden, as is the decorating of houses.' He jabbed a gloved finger in the direction of the house. 'Whatever your grandparents got away with, it cannot be permitted here.' With that, he marched off towards the front door.

'One day Christmas will be restored along with the King, but until then we must follow their rules. You don't want to see your father arrested, do you?' Agnes gave her children a tight smile.

'But at Owlcote…' William began.

'We are not at Owlcote now,' Agnes replied with uncharacteristic sharpness.

Chapter One

Marion bent over towards William. 'Measham Hall will be yours one day; just picture how magnificent it will be then,' she said encouragingly.

Once inside, however, the prospect was little improved despite the candles glowing in the wall sconces, for the light they threw out only revealed the accumulation of dirt and the loss of furniture. And though the fire had been lit in the hall, the cavernous room smelt damp and musty. The rush matting on the floor was caked in mud and released clouds of dust underfoot, which set them all sneezing. For the women, who had been seated inside the coach, the house felt miserably cold.

'Good evening, Sir Nicholas, Your Ladyship.' Norris hurried in from the kitchen, holding up a lantern. 'What an honour it is to be the first to welcome you home; I am only sorry the house could not be better prepared. The cook is here though and the kitchen-boy has lit fires in the parlour and some of the upper chambers. Indeed, you might find the parlour the most comfortable chamber to sit in.'

Sir Nicholas opened the door to the parlour and the others followed him in. It did not look very comfortable to Alethea. There were only three chairs, whose leather upholstery had been slashed and the horsehair stuffing pulled out. The only other furniture was an old, very scratched table and a cupboard. The shelves of the cupboard contained nothing but cobwebs. There were no pictures and above the spluttering fire, the mantlepiece was bare.

Alethea couldn't help thinking longingly of her grandparents' warm home, where everything was clean and ordered. All the fires would be burning brightly and the candles lit, the silver sparkling and the woodwork gleaming, and every chamber would smell of beeswax and bay leaves, frankincense and rosewater. Grandmother Ormerod was a stickler for cleanliness. The walls of her grandparents' hall were covered in finely woven tapestries telling familiar stories of knights on horseback and ladies at their looms, and in the corner was a chest filled with toys – drums, tops, balls and puppets – that she was allowed to play with every afternoon.

'I hope the silver we buried underneath the brewhouse is still there,' Agnes murmured.

'We'll look for that later,' Sir Nicholas said, taking a log from its basket and attempting to rejuvenate the fire. 'Lady Agnes and I will have our supper in here. Marion and the children can eat in the kitchen tonight,' he told Norris.

'We had better see that there are bedchambers fit for sleeping in.' Agnes's voice was high and strained.

'Norris can show you around. I'll make an inspection of the ground floor,' Sir Nicholas said gruffly.

'I'm sorry we haven't been able to clean the rooms properly yet,' Norris repeated anxiously, his long, skinny legs taking the stairs two at a time, so that he was forced to stop and wait for Agnes to precede him. 'Tom has swept the floors and we've done our best to purify the chambers.'

He led them along a passageway, opening the door to a large room that looked out onto the gardens below. An ornately carved bedstead stood against one wall, piled high with bedclothes.

'At least we know the bedding is clean,' Marion said as they surveyed the chamber.

Norris had brought the mattresses and blankets down from Lancashire, along with various other necessary items, all supplied by Agnes's parents.

Alethea was alarmed to see her mother's eyes filling with tears as she stared at the bare wooden bedposts.

'Did you find the bed-hangings stored somewhere?' Agnes asked Norris, a note of desperation in her voice.

'Alas, My Lady, we looked in every room, chest and cupboard, but could not discover them.'

Agnes hurried into the adjacent room and they heard her let out a terrible wail of lamentation. Running in after her, Alethea was brought up short by the sight of her mother standing in front of another empty bedstead, her arms outstretched.

Chapter One

'You were born on this bed,' she told her children. 'I delivered all my babies here, God bless their souls.' She ran her hand up and down one of the bed posts. 'The canopy, the valance and the curtains, I spun and embroidered them all when I was just a young girl dreaming of marriage.' Shaking her head, she gave a strange, mocking sort of laugh and gestured to the foot of the bed. 'The oak that stands in the garden at Owlcote, you know the one? It took up the whole of this curtain. I stitched birds into its branches, and rabbits nibbling the grass at its roots.' She walked round to the side of the bed, turning her head sorrowfully from side to side as she surveyed it. 'So many pretty blossoms and butterflies all worked so diligently in coloured crewel. You have no idea how many days I spent toiling with my needle to produce these hangings and now what has become of them? Brightening the dwelling of some black-suited Calvinist who lectures against adornment, no doubt.' She sank down onto the bed.

Marion sat down beside her, taking one of Agnes's hands into her own. 'We'll find out who's stolen them and petition to have all your beautiful drapery returned.'

'I should have taken them with me, but there was no time and we were only allowed to pack what we could carry.'

'It was heartless of them to force you from your home. Mrs Ormerod told me you had only just recovered from a miscarriage. It's a wonder you survived such rough treatment.' Marion shook her head.

William and Alethea watched in dismay as their mother, looking as small as a child beside the much larger Marion, laid her head against their nurse's shoulder and sobbed. They had never seen their mother cry before and had not thought her capable of such a passionate eruption. Alethea began to cry too, partly in sympathy and partly out of fright. William put his arm around her and they stood, leaning into one another as their previously imperturbable mother bawled like an infant.

When their father's heavy footsteps were heard in the next room, Agnes quickly rose to her feet, pulling a handkerchief from her sleeve and wiping away her tears.

'I don't know what possessed me.' Going over to the children, she planted a kiss on each of their heads. 'Pay me no mind, 'twas just a passing affliction.'

Sir Nicholas stood in the doorway. 'Things could be worse – they might have burnt the house down.' No one responded and he looked at Agnes. 'There's a cup of spiced wine in the parlour for you; that'll restore your spirits,' he told her. 'And if you're lucky' – he looked at the children – 'the cook might bake a minced pie; there is no law against that, nor against comfits.'

Alethea was very glad they were eating in the kitchen. When she, William and Marion emerged from the dark passageway that led off the hall, she felt as though they had stepped into a different house entirely. The large room glowed with warmth and industry and instead of the odours of mould and mice, it was filled with the smell of baking bread and roasting meat. Long wooden tables had been scrubbed clean and laid out with bunches of green herbs, mounds of vegetables, baskets of eggs and various types of fowl, their glossy feathers still to be plucked. Burnished pots and pans hung from the walls and the shelves were filled with pewter dishes, all gleaming in the candlelight as prettily as any household ornaments. Everything here appeared to be in its proper place and a sense of order reigned. Mother would be much happier in here than in the dark and dreary parlour, Alethea thought.

Looking up from the hare he was skinning, Tickell smiled broadly at the children. He had worked as the cook at Measham Hall before it was seized by Parliament and had been only too glad to return. Over the last few years he had been employed by a Parliamentarian general; the man had proved a stern and frugal master, one who preferred fasting to feasting. Now, despite Sir Nicholas's losses, Tickell hoped to resume the kind of cooking he enjoyed most, one that utilised his skills as a confectioner. For there was nothing Tickell enjoyed more than creating dainty sweetmeats and elaborate tarts and pies. There wasn't a creature or object Tickell could not recreate in pastry and though he was equally adept at baking, roasting and frying a range of fine meats for the Measham table, it was his pastry sculptures that had once been the talk of the county.

Tickell was, therefore, only too happy to comply with William's request for a minced pie. 'I was just thinking of the Christmas pies and how I might shape them. I plan on a large pie of neats' tongues shaped like the body of a lion, a quince pie for the head and then several curved minced pies round the beast, making up the Hawthorne crest. I've got in plenty of veal, and a good stock of fruit – dates, prunes, currants.' He ticked the ingredients off on his fingers. 'And spices too – cloves, mace, nutmeg, pepper. Times might be hard, but we'll have no shortage of fine savour.' He grinned conspiratorially at the children. The spices had been taken from the general's pantry, but since the general only liked plain food, Tickell didn't think they'd be missed.

'But we mustn't call them Christmas pies. Christmas is banned,' William replied solemnly.

'Understood.' Tickell winked at him and nodded.

Judging by Tickell's cheery demeanour, Alethea wasn't sure he did understand.

'There's no need to look so worried, little lady. Let's find you a sugarplum, shall we?' Tickell disappeared into the larder, appearing a few minutes later with two sugary comfits smelling of violets and aniseed. When these were eaten he told the children they must do all they could to help their mother in righting up the house. 'There's many women as would be weeping and wailing at the destruction, but not our good lady. She's a saint, your mother, and God will reward her for her fortitude.' Lady Agnes's presence was another reason why Tickell had been happy to return to Measham Hall. He worshipped his mistress with the devotion of a romantic knight.

'Mother has been crying,' Alethea told him. Seeing the concerned look on Tickell's face, she added, 'But only a little.'

'It would take a heart of stone not to shed a few tears at the state of the place. And that's all the more reason to assist her now.' Tickell returned to his hares, wanting to get them done so that he could go on to make a selection of minced pies so fine they would bring some joy into His Lady's heart.

→ Chapter Two ←

22nd December 1653

Cakes and Ale
To make a Spice Cake
Take one bushel of Flower, six pound of Butter, eight pound of Currants, two pints of Cream, a pottle of Milk, half a pint of good Sack, two pound of Sugar, two ounces of Mace, one ounce of Nutmegs, one ounce of Ginger, twelve yolks, two whites, take the Milk and Cream, and stir it all the time that it boils, put your Butter into a basin, and put your hot seething Milk to it, and melt all the Butter in it, and when it is blood warm temper the Cake, put not your Currants in till you have made the paste, you must have some Ale yeast, and forget not Salt.

(Elizabeth Grey, *A True Gentlewoman's Delight*)

Agnes rose while it was still dark, slipping out of bed without so much as lifting the blankets in case a cold draught should wake her sleeping husband. Lighting a taper in the embers of the bedroom fire, she tiptoed downstairs to kneel by the hearth in the empty parlour. The fire had long gone out, but there was still some warmth left in the room. Besides, she did not mind the cold pushing its icy fingers into her flesh; she needed this mortification of the body to bring her passions under control. Her outburst the previous day had been as shocking to Agnes as it had been to her children and now, pressing her knees into the cold tiles, she applied herself to seeking God's forgiveness.

She was in the habit of praying before daybreak. Sometimes she feared she treasured this time alone with God so much it had become an act of self-regard instead of worship. But her early morning meditations fortified her, enabling her to travel through the day with the poise so admired by those around her. Without this time of private prayer she did not think she would be able to fulfil all the duties required of a wife and mother. Now she reminded herself that the Lord never imposed on anyone a burden heavier than they could carry. She must show fortitude in the face of adversity and provide a good model for her children to follow. God had brought her husband back to her and restored them to their rightful home; she should not be so ungrateful as to covet the comfort and ease of her parents' house. And her parents had been very generous in bestowing them with ample provisions. They had enough cured and smoked meats to feed them for several weeks, plenty of hogsheads of beer and of wine, along with enough tapers to see them through the longest nights. She must count her blessings instead of bemoaning her lot.

Agnes prayed for Sir Nicholas to turn likewise to God for guidance and support so that he might not suffer so much grievance and torment at his worldly losses. She entreated God to open her husband's eyes to the comfort that might be found in Christ, so that his choler might be soothed and his melancholy alleviated. Sir Nicholas was too irascible for her to risk making these entreaties directly, so she could only beseech God on his behalf, hoping his heart might soften enough to receive such blessings as were there for him.

Although it was Agnes's petitions to Parliament and to the local Sequestration Committee that had been instrumental in regaining the Measham estates and ensuring her husband's safe passage home, she took no pride in her achievements. For instead of being glad her efforts had proved successful, Sir Nicholas seemed only to resent her for them. Of course, it was hard for a man to be forced to rely on his wife, especially when it came to his financial affairs. The world had, as many said, been turned upside down and women were often accused of wearing their husband's breeches when, in fact, all they were doing was defending their property so that it might be passed on to their sons. But Agnes refused to allow such insults to grieve her, for she understood that just as Christ had endured the insults cast at him, 'if, when ye do well, and suffer for it, ye take it patiently, this is acceptable with God'.

Sir Nicholas was disappointed to wake alone and wondered where his wife had gone. He thought he might find her in the kitchen directing the housekeeping, but as he passed the parlour door, he glimpsed her kneeling by the empty grate, her rosary clasped between her hands. Her eyes were closed and her lips moved in prayer. Agnes had always been devout, but had become more so during his absence. At times he feared she would be happier in a convent than by his side. He stood for a moment, wondering whether he ought to join her, but her prayers seemed of a private nature, so he walked away quietly.

It saddened him that she had not even lit the fire. Did she think them so impoverished they could not spare the fuel? Once they had got the house back to how it should be, she could have her own room again, along with a maid who would light the fires while her mistress was still deep in slumber.

In the meantime he needed to survey what was left of his woods and park. After stopping in the kitchen for a draught of ale, Sir Nicholas went straight out to the stables and saddled a horse. As he rode out, the sense of joy he felt at being back on his own land again battled with dread of what depredations he might discover.

A great deal of his land had been sold off by Parliament, some of it to a neighbour he had once considered a good friend. Sir Peverell had taken the side of the Roundheads during the late wars and they had rewarded him well for betraying his King and country, letting him have the Measham land for a pittance. Sir Nicholas had exchanged several letters with Peverell, but the weasel refused to return it to him, not even when he offered to pay for what was rightfully his. The man Sir Nicholas had spent many hours hunting and drinking with said he could not give the land up on credit when there was no assurance Sir Nicholas would ever have the means to pay back the debt.

It was true he desperately needed to raise some revenue, for he had returned to England quite penniless and could no longer trade on his name and reputation, which, though it had once been highly esteemed, was worthless in the new Commonwealth. He'd been forced to borrow from his father-in-law, an uncomfortable position since he was beholden enough to the man already.

He wished Crewe were with him. He had grown up alongside Crewe, whose father had been their steward. Crewe had fought with him and fled with him after their defeat on Marston Moor. He had tried to persuade his friend and servant to return to England with him, but Crewe refused to take the oath of engagement and swore he would only come back once the King was on his throne again.

At least John Thornly, his old bailiff, was still at the Grange. Thornly was a trustworthy fellow, who would tell him exactly how many deer were left in the park, what numbers of hares, partridges and grouse remained, how much timber had been felled and whether the river was still teeming with waterfowl, fish and otters.

As soon as Sir Nicholas had mounted his horse and cantered off, the house itself, along with everyone in it, seemed to breathe a sigh of relief, or so it seemed to William. He was reassured to see his mother had regained her customary composure and was calmly making an inventory of everything that needed repairing and which items would have to be brought in to replace those things they could not do

Chapter Two

without. She was being assisted in this by Marion, which left William and Alethea at liberty to do as they pleased.

'Come with me,' he whispered to Alethea, who was staring longingly out of their bedroom window.

'Are we going outside?' she asked eagerly.

William shook his head. 'We haven't explored the house properly yet.' He was eager to see the rest of the building that would one day be his.

Alethea followed him up the creaking wooden staircase to the long gallery. William had vague memories of playing skittles and chasing tennis balls along acres of smooth wooden floor. He was disappointed then to find it not so large or grand as it had been in his memory. The ivy covering the windows kept out the bright winter sunlight and the shaded room was cold and dusty. The unlit fireplaces smelt of piss and the air was still tainted with the sweat of the soldiers who had slept there. The toys and ornaments had all gone; only a few paintings remained on the walls. One, a portrait of a man in a ruff, had been crudely drawn over with charcoal so that a pair of devil's horns protruded from his head and the words 'Satan's ass' emerged from his mouth.

'I wish Father had let us remain at Owlcote,' Alethea lamented.

'Father said we must reestablish ourselves here, as a family, in case they take it from us again.' But William couldn't help picturing the greenery brought in to decorate every beam and mantlepiece at Owlcote and how he would have helped his grandfather to gather and place it there.

Both children stood in silence, remembering the fierce argument between their father and grandfather. Grandfather Ormerod wanted his son-in-law to wait until the spring, as any sane man would, or if he could not stay that long, at least until after Twelfth Night, before dragging his family back to a ruined house.

The wind was picking up; it had begun to whistle in the chimneys and the branches of the ivy were scratching at the windowpanes.

'What's that?' Alethea pointed with alarm at a hairy lump, huddled against the far wall.

Drawing his sword, William advanced on the creature, though he suspected it was already dead. It didn't move as he got closer and he poked it with the tip of his sword. Nothing stirred. He plunged his sword into the shapeless mass then raised it aloft. A tattered blanket hung limply from his blade. William let out the breath he had been holding with a mixture of gratitude and disappointment. He wanted to impress his little sister with his daring, but was relieved not to have been overpowered by a ravenous dog or an angry soldier.

'I am the master of Measham Hall,' he shouted, waving his sword like an ensign with a banner.

'The soldiers must have left it. Don't touch it, it's probably full of fleas,' Alethea warned him.

He shook his sword, trying to dislodge the hempen rag, and was forced to step on a corner of it to pull it off. A mouse ran out from under the folds and scuttled away into a hole in the wainscot. William jumped and almost dropped his sword. Alethea screamed.

'It's just a mouse, silly.'

Alethea frowned but said nothing. She hadn't seen the mouse; it was William leaping into the air that had alarmed her.

'Watch out!' William came running at her, a torn strip of blanket dangling from his sword.

Her shrieks as she raced the length of the room with William in pursuit brought both their mother and Marion running upstairs.

'You deserve a good whipping, the pair of you,' Marion cried. 'Scaring your mother like that.' Marion's chest heaved as she tried to catch her breath.

'I have a more fitting punishment,' Agnes said more calmly. 'You can fetch brooms, a bucket and mop and give this place a clean.'

William looked aghast. 'That is not proper work for a gentleman.'

'Think of it as a penance.' Agnes patted his shoulder. 'Holy men, such as monks and friars, do not consider any task beneath their dignity, for any work undertaken in God's honour is a blessed one.'

Alethea wanted to ask about work not done in God's honour. She would be sweeping the floor under her mother's command and couldn't see what difference it made to God whether the room was dirty or not, but William appeared to have been won over by this argument and was bowing to their mother.

'I'll ask Norris to bring up some wood and get the fires lit in here,' Agnes said, surveying the gallery. 'That at least will purge the foul odours.'

They were halfway down the stairs when there was a knocking at the hall doors. The four of them stopped, all but Alethea afraid the soldiers might have returned. William twisted the handle of his sword between his hands. Marion crossed herself and began to pray. Agnes stood very still and very straight. She was glad Sir Nicholas was not at home; he had become so quick to anger and she didn't know how he would react to a visit from soldiers or Parliament-men. It would be easier for her to negotiate in her husband's absence, something she had become accustomed to doing when he fled overseas. The knocking, though loud enough to be heard, was not as hard or rapid as that of a militia demanding entry, however. It was more akin to a polite tapping than a belligerent hammering.

Since the other three appeared to be frozen on their respective stairs, Alethea was about to ask if she should run in search of Norris, when the man himself appeared, his long legs striding across the hall. He unbolted and opened the door at a leisurely and ceremonious pace.

'Valentine Evans, at your service.' Sweeping his hat off his head, the man on the doorstep gave a low bow, his arms extended sideways. He was dressed in gold and scarlet velvet and the bright colours of his clothes seemed to glow against the drabness of the hall.

'May I introduce my small troupe, lately in the employment of Lord Ingrams?'

Evans spun round on his heel, gesturing to the band of men behind him, who all began bowing and nodding, bobbing their heads like a flock of pigeons. But only Alethea was amused; Norris was regarding them with a particularly disdainful expression.

'Having been unexpectedly turned out of His Lordship's manor we find ourselves forced to seek our fortunes on the road,' Evans continued without pausing. 'We were informed that a noble family of good Christians had lately returned to this house and wish to offer our services in celebrating the nativity of our saviour's birthday.'

'You are mistaken, sir, we do not require your services here,' Norris said firmly, about to shut the door.

'Pray stay your hand a moment,' Evans called out. 'I see your lady on the stair and beseech an audience with her, for she stands as lovely as Diana, queen of the heavens, mistress of the stars, floating up there amongst the spheres.' Evans knelt so that his knee rested on the threshold and Norris could not close the door. 'How fortunate are we to behold such radiance. Oh shine it upon us a little longer, fair lady, and fulfil the claims of charity due to the season.' He lifted his hands in supplication towards Agnes. 'And in return we can entertain your household, My Lady, restoring that merriment sorely lacking in the current times.' He thrust out an arm from beneath his crimson cloak. 'I see your children there are in want of some Christmas cheer – we will return the smiles to their faces and the laughter to your halls.'

'Alas, we are not in a position to welcome you,' Agnes replied sadly, not moving from where she stood. 'The current times, to which you refer, make it impossible.'

A woman stepped out from the group on the doorstep and leant forward over the kneeling Evans. 'Oh do not prove as cold as the harsh winds outside, My Lady,' she cried. And indeed, as she spoke, the wind, or one of the fellows behind her, whipped back her cape to reveal a young child in her arms.

The child peeped up at them from beneath a red hood. Her dark eyes were as round and plaintive as a puppy dog's and began to fill with tears as she let out a plaintive sob.

'The sable curtains of the night are descending on this all too brief winter's day; do not abandon us to the icy wilderness,' Evans implored.

The child's sobs increased to a steady wail.

Evans's appeal to her Christian charity tugged painfully at Agnes's conscience. Christ's words rang in her ears – 'Behold I have set before thee an open door and no man can shut it'. Her parents had always observed the traditional Christmas hospitality, keeping their house open to any who came seeking alms. It sat ill with her to be forced into meanness by the puritan party.

'Norris will show you to the kitchen, where the cook will furnish you with victuals, but then you must go on your way again.' Agnes descended the stairs, followed by her little retinue.

'Your Ladyship is most gracious.' Evans touched his forehead to the floor before jumping nimbly to his feet. 'May I introduce my wife, Mrs Susanna Evans, and our daughter, Fortuna.'

Mrs Evans curtseyed and set Fortuna on the ground, where, to the surprise of her audience, the girl threw off her cape, performing a graceful curtsey followed by a somersault and a back-caper. When she had finished tumbling, she ran to Agnes, throwing her arms around Agnes's legs.

'*Merci, grazie*, thanking you kindly, gracious lady,' she lisped.

Agnes laughed despite herself, and stroked the girl's head. 'Well, you are a clever little tumbler.'

'Would you care to see me dance on a rope?' Fortuna asked with great seriousness.

'Oh please can we, madam?' Alethea asked her mother.

'Let us see them fed, first.'

Several men, ranging in age and size, had followed the Evanses into the hall and Agnes did not want Sir Nicholas to walk straight into the midst of them. It was, as Evans had pointed out, growing dark and Nicholas was likely to return at any moment. They appeared to be well-mannered, respectful fellows and she had no qualms about allowing them into the kitchen, but their courtesy was unlikely to placate her husband.

She and Norris ushered the troupe into the kitchen, where Tickell was shouting at the kitchen-boy to keep turning the spit. A haunch of beef, brought with them from Owlcote, was roasting over the fire, or at least, one side of it was. Tickell stared at the visitors with a mixture of concern and pleasure. If Her Ladyship had invited more guests to dine, or men to serve, it was not for him to question. The former would mean more people to appreciate his cooking, the latter, more help in the kitchen, which was sorely needed. Though quite how he was to feed them all was another matter.

Agnes answered his ponderings by ordering him to provide beer, bread and cheese, along with whatever else he had in ready supply. Their visitors would not be staying long, she insisted. She and Marion helped Tickell to assemble the food. Agnes kept a careful eye on their provisions, calculating how generous they could afford to be as she sat their guests at the long kitchen table.

William inserted himself on the bench beside two of the younger players. One of his favourite activities at his grandparents' had been reading and enacting plays. Sometimes friends of his grandfather joined them and they all took parts, reading them out in turn. William too had been allowed small parts. Once, his grandfather had even taken him to an inn to see a secret performance of a drama. It had been the most thrilling occasion of his life to be transported to a world of heroics and poetry. He had never laughed so much as then, seeing the clowns chasing each other round the room and making fun of the pompous puritan preacher – who was an actor in disguise, of course, not a real puritan. This too had astonished him, the magical transformation of a man into an entirely different person.

His grandfather had made William promise not to breathe a word of their excursion to anyone; telling him that if news of their performance spread, the actors could be arrested. And there was no need to frighten his mother and grandmother unnecessarily; besides, ladies, being naturally more cautious, would only chastise him for exposing his grandson to danger. This secrecy had enhanced the escapade in William's mind and he felt very proud to have been trusted by his grandfather to accompany him.

And now the kitchen at Measham Hall was full of players, perhaps they might even put on a play. William questioned the boys next to him, wanting to know everything about the parts they played and which they liked the best. The youths, who introduced themselves as Stephen Wallis and Michael Lowin, explained that they took the female characters and began to regale William with some of their speeches.

Chapter Two

Alethea stood, watching and listening with shy fascination, as Michael turned himself from a tragic princess to a blushing maiden. He and Stephen acted out a love scene with such passion, everyone in the kitchen applauded. In response, Valentine Evans took to his feet to deliver a soliloquy with great gusto, his plump lips trembling along with his chin, as tears dropped from his eyes.

It was at this moment, Sir Nicholas arrived in the kitchen. He had been alerted to the presence of visitors by the horse and cart tied up outside. Now he watched the scene before him with disbelief. The rest of the household were so enraptured with the performers they didn't even notice his presence.

Agnes, who was always guarded and cautious with him now, appeared suddenly like the young maiden he'd wed twelve years ago, before the country began tearing itself apart in civil strife. A smile played over her parted lips, and her cheeks, warmed by the kitchen fire and the company, had gained a rosy hue. She had clear, soft skin and never wore cosmetics, unlike the women who travelled with the exiled Court, but this natural rouge enlivened her pallid complexion. Her usually still oval face, had become charmingly animated as she responded to the actors with gasps and laughter, wrinkling her nose and pouting at a bawdy reference.

The children too had lost the apprehensive expressions they'd worn since his return. It irritated Nicholas, the way they looked at him as though he were an ogre come to devour them. His daughter especially – he could hardly get a coherent word out of the wench. He'd feared she was half-witted, but Agnes assured him this was not the case. It was only when he'd witnessed her chatter to her grandparents that he conceded she had all her faculties. Of course he expected his children to treat him with the deference owed a father, but he had also anticipated a sense of kinship with them. During his five years of banishment he had thought often of his family at home, imagining a brave and clever son who would be eager to demonstrate his skills and learning to his father, and a pretty daughter who would run to him to be petted and cherished. But it seemed the Ormerods had spoilt their grandchildren and Alethea shrank from him, while his son was a milksop.

Sometimes, in more lonely hours abroad, he had envied those men who'd brought their families with them overseas, but seeing also the trouble and expense it put them to, when they could scarcely afford to feed themselves, he'd thought it wiser to leave his family in England. Now, though, his own wife and the children he'd sired seemed like strangers to him. Or perhaps he was the stranger, standing in the shadows like a ghost at a wake, instead of acting as the host in his own house.

Although he had entered the kitchen intending to see these uninvited guests off his premises, Sir Nicholas found himself waiting to hear the rest of the clown's speech. It was like being back with the itinerant Court, where, despite the lack of money, there had always been entertainment of one kind or another.

Hearing a cough at his side, he turned to find the cook holding out a cup of spiced wine and a plate laden with slices of cake and cheese. Taking both, he nodded at Tickell. He might as well enjoy a moment's respite, he thought, before having to take on the role of tyrant and enforce the law.

He had drunk a second cup of wine before he finally called attention to his presence. Poor Agnes nearly fell off her stool when she saw him emerge from the back of the kitchen. Hurrying over to him, she held up her hands in supplication. He stopped her as she began to explain who the company were.

'I can see you are talented fellows,' he told them. 'But now you have enjoyed our bounty it is time for you to be on your way.'

'Perhaps they might stay one night?' Agnes said softly, having been won over by Evans's oratory.

'I have only lately recovered my estate; I am not going to risk losing it again.' Sir Nicholas thumped his cup down on the table beside him.

'Please, sir, may I show you my dancing first?' a child's voice piped up.

Fortuna had been sleeping curled up by her mother like a cat and Sir Nicholas had not noticed her before. Now she skipped across the kitchen towards him, somersaulting in the air before landing at his feet and taking hold of his hands. Each member of his family held their breath, expecting a furious response. Sir Nicholas looked down at the child; she really was as pretty as an elfin princess with her black curls and dainty form. In response she smiled up at him, dimples forming in her olive cheeks.

'Kind gentleman, would you like to see me put twoscore threads through the eye of a needle?'

The rest of his family were astonished when Sir Nicholas burst out laughing.

'That I should like to see, but I tell you this, little maid, I have seen a similar trick performed on horseback in Paris.'

Fortuna's eyes widened. 'I can do it standing on a rope and if you allow me to practise on one of your horses I am sure I can thread a needle on horseback too.' She squeezed his fingers, which she still clasped in her small hands.

'Well, you are quite the fearless one,' Nicholas observed good-humouredly.

'Shall I dance for you now?'

Two of the players were already on their feet and pulling a thick rope out of a basket. When Sir Nicholas nodded, they placed themselves at either end of the kitchen, holding the rope up over their shoulders so that it was stretched taut. Fortuna climbed nimbly up Michael's back and onto his shoulders, then, extending a leg straight in front of her, she stepped out onto the rope. It quivered beneath her slippered feet but she didn't appear the least afraid as she stared straight ahead with a look of calm concentration.

Alethea was transfixed. Fortuna must be younger than she was and yet far exceeded her in both skill and bravery. Alethea trembled in the presence of her own father, whereas this girl treated him like a fond uncle.

When Fortuna began to dance, every member of the household gasped with astonished delight. Her feet seemed to fly above the rope she trod so lightly. Her short rose-pink skirts and creamy petticoats fluttered about her little legs as if she was indeed a fairy dressed in flower petals, hovering in the air above them. She stopped in the middle of the rope and felt inside the purse hanging at her waist. Drawing out a needle, she held it up for all to see that there was nothing attached to it. Then she pulled thread after thread out from the purse and pushed each one through the eye of the needle. When they had counted forty threads she stuck the needle into the purse and proceeded on to the other end of the rope. Instead of climbing down or turning round, she moved backwards along the rope without taking a single misstep, until she arrived back on Michael's shoulders. Letting go of the rope, he stretched up his arms and lifted her down, placing her carefully back on the ground. Fortuna ran to Sir Nicholas and, pulling the needle out of the purse, presented it to him with a bow.

He chuckled as he examined it. 'Well, that was quite a feat, my tumbling lass. I've not seen a better performance in France or the Low Countries.'

'Not even on horseback?'

'Well...' Sir Nicholas's brow furrowed. 'That trick was performed by a grown woman. I should like to see what you can do when you're her age.'

Fortuna gazed up at him with eyes so dark they resembled two pools of ink. 'Then will you let us stay now, sir?'

'Until you are grown? I think not,' he answered with a mocking laugh.

'If I may make my petition, Sir Nicholas.' Evans came forward, bowing. 'Valentine Evans at your humble service.'

Agnes placed a tentative hand on Nicholas's arm, but he paid no more attention to it than he would to a fly. He was looking hard at Evans, who had launched into a lyrical and poignant speech on behalf of his company.

'Mr Norris told me how few hands you have here. Should any militias call, which is most unlikely at this time of year, especially when snow is expected to fall, we will take on the roles of servants employed in repairing your illustrious home. My boys all make good serving-men,' Evans concluded. Moving in a sprightly fashion around his players, he clapped two of the youngest on their backs. 'Stephen Wallis and Michael Lowin have played a variety of domestics, from ladies' maids to washerwomen.' Stephen and Michael simpered as they curtseyed. 'While Robert Hart here makes a very good nursemaid; did you not play fair Juliet's nurse to great acclaim?' Evans gestured to the short, round-faced, bald-headed man standing next to Alethea.

Hart placed a hand on Alethea's shoulder, telling her with great sincerity, 'Thou wast the prettiest babe that ere I nursed.' His eyes wrinkled up like currants topping the puffed-up buns of his cheeks and Alethea wished he was her nurse, he seemed so kind and merry.

'They can be footboys, pages and messengers too,' Evans continued. 'In addition to taking the heroic parts, Mr Alleyn has played many fine and loyal valets, some who save their masters from great misfortune.' He gestured to a well-formed young man who was still sitting near the fire. On hearing his name, Alleyn rose gracefully and gave an elegant bow. 'Myself and Abraham Palmes' – Evans slapped the last player on the back – 'can take the parts of loyal retainers, stewards, sergeants, valets, grooms and the like.'

Sir Nicholas raised his hands as if in defeat. 'We are in need of most of these servants; perhaps you would like to take on the parts in reality.'

'If the puritan party continue to govern with such strictness we might well become your willing hirelings, sire,' Evans responded.

'There is a cold and bitter wind out.' Sir Nicholas surveyed the occupants of the kitchen. 'Out of respect for the season, you may lodge here this night, but you must move on tomorrow, first thing.'

Cries of gratitude resounded round the room. Palmes, a plain-looking man with a sober demeanour, set the younger players to work cleaning up after their supper, before offering his assistance to Norris in preparing their quarters. In a corner of the kitchen, Alleyn had taken out his lute and was playing a plaintive air. Fortuna had gone back to sleep and now Alethea and William dozed beside her. Marion was too enthralled by the music to take the children up to bed. Agnes was laughing at a story told by Evans with interjections from his wife and Robert Hart. Sir Nicholas told Tickell to fetch another bottle of wine. He might as well enjoy the players' entertainments for this one night.

✦ Chapter Three ✦

23rd December 1653

A dish of Larks
Pull your Larks and draw them, and spit them on a small spit, with a slice of Bacon, and a Sage-leaf between each Lark: being roasted, dish them up with a sauce made of the juyce of two or three Oranges, Claret, and a little sliced Ginger; then set it on the fire a little while, and beat it up with a piece of Butter, and so serve them up. With the same sauce you may broil your Larks on a Gridiron, opening their breasts and laying them abroad.

(*The Compleat Cook*)

I t was not yet light when Alethea woke the next morning and she lay listening for the church bells that would tell her the night was past. Marion was snoring gently, her lanky form shrouded in blankets like a range of mountains beneath a layer of snow. Marion was much more agreeable asleep than she was when awake and it was tempting to remain curled up against her back, cocooned in the warmth emanating from her body, but Alethea was desperate to see the players again before they left. She had been praying all night for a heavy snowfall that would cut off the roads, for she was sure her father wouldn't turn them out in such conditions.

As soon as she heard the bell toll six times, she slipped out from under the bedclothes. The air, like icy water, stung her legs and face. Pulling a rug from the end of the bed, she wrapped it round herself and tiptoed to the window, where she carefully opened one of the shutters. Marion grunted, but soon resumed her steady snoring.

The windowpanes were patterned with hoar-frost. She blew steamy breath over one of them, rubbing away the pretty tendrils of ice with the corner of her blanket. Outside, the box hedges glittered in the moonlight like sweetmeats rolled in powdered sugar. The naked branches of the trees were likewise dusted in white. Would a hard frost be enough to detain the players?

Alethea listened carefully for any sounds emanating from the long gallery, which, having served as a dormitory for soldiers, now housed the actors. All she could hear was the scratching of a mouse behind the wainscot. She would do her best to dress herself so that she could go down to the kitchen, where Tickell was sure to be up and the fires lit.

There was a rustling from the truckle-bed on which William was sleeping and his head emerged suddenly from beneath his blankets like a mole out of the ground.

'What are you doing?' he asked.

'Getting up,' she whispered back. 'Can you help me tie my laces?'

Rubbing the sleep from his eyes, William stumbled out of bed and shivered. 'It's too cold. Can't you wait until the fires have been lit?' He hopped from one foot to the other.

Marion murmured something. They turned and looked at her, but she seemed to be sleeping. 'Oh my love,' she muttered, stretching and rolling onto her other side.

Both children began to giggle and were soon doubled up, their hands pressed over their mouths in an attempt to stifle their laughter.

'It'll be warm in the kitchen and Tickell will give us a draught of small beer and some bread and butter,' Alethea told William once she had recovered.

Chapter Three

She picked up his doublet and breeches, which had been left in a folded pile on the floor, there not being any furniture except the beds, and handed them to him. Without bothering to change their chemises, they pulled their stockings on first, eager to warm their icy toes. Even Alethea was able to tie her garters and step into her red woollen petticoat and bodice, but then she had to wait while William clambered into his clothes. He seemed to take an age to do up all the buttons, waving her away when she tried to help.

Once he was dressed, he dropped the rest of Alethea's petticoats over her head, one by one, tying them deftly at the back, before lacing up her bodice. He had watched Marion dressing his little sister enough times to remember how it was done and was rather proud of his skill at tying knots.

Grabbing their jackets, they tiptoed across the floorboards, grinning at each other in triumph when they made it out of the room before Marion stirred again. As they passed the parlour they could hear their mother's voice reciting her prayers. William paused, tempted to join her, but Alethea was tugging at his sleeve and the lure of the kitchen fire and a full belly temporarily overcame his desire to please his mother.

All the bread had been eaten the previous night and Tickell was waiting for a new batch to bake, but he gave them some hot mutton broth and a roast lark each, wrapped in a slice of bacon, which was even better as far as Willam was concerned. They sat on stools in front of the fire, basking in the heat it threw out.

'Let's go outside and check on the weather,' Alethea suggested eagerly as soon as they had finished their breakfast.

But William shook his head. He had no desire to tramp about in the half-dark, growing cold and damp, especially when he could see perfectly well through the window that the ground was frozen hard. He was concerned too about their mother. It had filled him with joy to see her laughing again at the antics of the players, but this brief happiness could not dispel the memory of her anguish the day before. William shared a close bond with his mother and it distressed him to see her suffering. Despite being only nine years of age, his position as the eldest child during his father's long absence had encouraged not only a strong sense of duty, but also a protectiveness towards Agnes.

'You can go into the garden,' he told his sister. 'I have matters to attend to here.'

Alethea was disappointed not to have William's company, but she guessed that he was going to share in their mother's devotions and, having no desire to spend any more time in prayer than was strictly necessary, she headed for the back door.

A band of rosy gold was stretching itself upwards across the sky, bringing the trees on the hill into sharp relief. It felt too cold for snow, but when she ran across the stiff, crackling grass and down to the road, Alethea found it too was encrusted with ice. The water in the ditches was frozen so hard it could not be broken by stamping on it, nor by sticks poked or stones thrown at it. Slipping, she almost ended up on her bottom, just managing to right herself in time, a feat for which she congratulated herself. She knew only too well the sort of punishment Marion would mete out to her if she returned with wet skirts.

'It will be very hard for them to travel on this,' she declared with satisfaction. 'Worse even than snow.'

'You are testing the ground, are you?'

Alethea was startled to hear her father's voice and turned to find him standing behind her, surveying the scene.

'The ice is very thick, sir,' she answered cautiously.

'When I was in Antwerp I saw people sliding on the frozen river. They have special boots for it with blades attached, called *schaatsen*, and can go very fast. Some slide so gracefully it is as if they are dancing.'

Alethea watched her father, who was staring out across the land with an absent expression, as if he had been transported back to that foreign place where the people could glide over the ice in their magical boots. She wished he had brought her back a pair.

'Anyway, your mother has persuaded me to let the players stay another day or two, for the sake of Christian charity. We're as hard to reach as we are to leave and can only hope that affords us some protection.'

Alethea was made so happy by this news she temporarily forgot her fear of her father and clapped her hands together, smiling. 'It is only two days until Christmas Day,' she sang.

'But we do not name it,' he reminded her with a warning look. 'Your mother and brother are praying; you'd best go and join them.'

It occurred to Alethea that she had never seen her father pray and she was tempted to ask him about this, but she didn't want to anger him. She leapt from the road onto the grassy verge, which was easier to walk on, grasping a branch to steady herself. To her surprise her father laughed.

'You'll have to ask the little gypsy girl for some lessons in vaulting,' he called to her.

She wasn't sure if he meant this seriously or not, so she just gave a short bow in reply. Her father nodded at her and she sped off towards the house, glad to have escaped a chiding for her tom-boyish conduct. It was the sort of behaviour that often got her into trouble with her mother and grandmother.

Sir Nicholas watched her go. At least his daughter liked to get outdoors; she took after him in that. He would have preferred to see his son outside too, running about instead of kneeling beside Agnes. He could hardly fault his wife for her piety, but he feared the influence of too much religion on his heir. Agnes's father was a man of soft affections and William needed the example of a proper man. Perhaps it had been a mistake to leave his son with the Ormerods, but then, if he had taken William with him, the boy might equally have picked up unwholesome habits from all the trash that trailed after the King. The younger exiled Englishmen had earnt themselves bad reputations for duelling and drinking, making them unwelcome in many Continental towns. Nicholas would not have wanted to expose William to that either. He didn't want his son growing up to be a libertine.

He surveyed the wintry garden with dissatisfaction. Even at this dead time of year it was evident how overgrown and unkempt the trees and shrubs were. Heaps of decaying brown leaves had buried all the plots where vegetables might grow. Everything needed taking in order, including his son. William was his mother's darling all right. It was only to be expected, Nicholas supposed, William being their only surviving son. Agnes had taken the loss of the other two hard, blaming herself for incurring the Lord's displeasure. He hoped to get her with child again soon. Given all her praying, God would surely reward them with another healthy boy child. It wasn't just the need to have an heir in reserve; the memory of Agnes's face, radiant with pride and joy as she watched her little boy take his first steps, had brought him much solace when he was abroad. She deserved to know such happiness again.

'Where have you been, bush-head?' Marion cried, grabbing Alethea and hauling her into their chamber. 'Look at the state of your hair!' Taking a brush, she began dragging it through Alethea's tangled locks.

Alethea screamed and Marion switched to beating her backside with the same instrument of torture, though this at least was less painful due to the thickness of Alethea's petticoats.

'Sir Nicholas said I am to join my mother at prayers,' Alethea shouted between whacks.

'Well, you are too late for that. Dame Agnes is upstairs speaking to the players.' Tiring of her exercise, Marion put the brush down and shook her weary arms. 'We must make you presentable to her,' she said with a defeated air.

Alethea looked down at her skirts. They were less muddy than usual thanks to the frozen ground and she had remembered to remove her dirty boots.

'This will have to do.' Marion slapped a clean linen cap on Alethea's head, tying the strings tightly under her chin.

Alethea began to pull at the ribbons, which were cutting into her neck, but seeing her nurse's expression, desisted and smiled demurely at Marion instead.

'Come along, we'll see what entertainment the players can offer us,' Marion said, her anger forgotten in her eagerness to mingle with the actors again.

Alethea had to run to keep up with her, as Marion bounded up the stairs to the gallery. She had never known her nurse to be so energetic and felt as though she were racing a horse. Marion had lifted her skirts and her brawny legs pounded up the steps like a charging courser, so that Alethea was tempted to shout 'Whoa!'

This was unnecessary, however, as Marion came to an abrupt halt when they reached the long room. 'Well, this is an improvement,' she exclaimed.

The floorboards had been swept and mopped, the fires lit and the cupboards dusted. The yeasty odours had been banished by the woodsmoke and replaced with a herbal fragrance that was drifting down from the posies of bay leaves and rosemary that Fortuna was hanging from the rafters. She was assisted in this task by Palmes, on whose shoulders she balanced. They sang as they worked and Alethea wished that she could join in, even though Palmes was singing out of tune. She looked around for William and spotted him at the far end of the gallery, playing at sword-fighting with another of the actors.

Her mother was talking earnestly to Mrs Evans. She turned at Alethea's approach and gave her a warm smile. Agnes's face in repose could take on a severe expression, but when she smiled it was as if the sun had come out on an overcast day and everyone fortunate enough to behold it basked in her smile's radiance. Alethea felt as though summer had come early she was so pleased to see her mother cheerful again.

'Haven't they worked wonders? Sir Nicholas will be most impressed.' Agnes beamed as she came towards them.

'He will indeed, madam. Can they start on the parlour next?' Marion asked, only half in jest.

'They are going to entertain us tomorrow with a performance in honour of the King and all who fought for him,' Agnes told her.

'Is that wise, madam?' Marion asked quietly.

'No one but ourselves will see it and I hope it might raise my husband's spirits.' Agnes also lowered her voice. 'It is our duty to remind Sir Nicholas that the cause he sacrificed so much for has not been forgotten. I hope this might lift the melancholy from his heart and signal to him that all is not lost.' She glanced around the gallery. 'The message will of course be hidden, so that it is clear only to those who understand it.'

'Even so, My Lady, any form of play-acting is prohibited and should the soldiers come, they'll clap us all in irons.' Marion's eyes had grown wide with fear and her voice quivered.

'I have prayed all night for guidance,' Agnes replied calmly. 'Is it not our Christian duty to celebrate the birth of our Saviour? Tomorrow we will expunge all remnants of the rebels from our home and call in the blessings of the Lord. The best masques convey a moral tale, one that can improve all who participate, actors and audience alike.' She closed her eyes for a moment and both Marion and Alethea knew that it was pointless to argue any further. Once Agnes had referred to God there was no dissuading her.

Despite sharing some of her nurse's anxiety, the excitement was rising through Alethea's body and she couldn't help but skip from one foot to the other as she watched Mrs Evans pulling brightly coloured costumes out of a chest. It had been unbearable to think of the short winter days all passing uniformly with nothing to relieve the dreariness. Now her mother had restored the joy of a holiday. Perhaps, if their performance pleased Father, the players might even be allowed to remain until Twelfth Night, when there were bound to be further revels.

'I have been telling Mrs Evans to include a piece for you to sing, Alethea. A Christmas carol to finish the celebrations with. Should we be interrupted, which I don't believe we will, you can always switch to a psalm; there are a couple you know by heart, are there not? The sixty-first psalm for instance; that's one for the Puritans.'

Alethea felt all the blood draining from her head right down into her toes. 'I don't believe I sing well enough, madam.'

'Pish, pish.' Marion seized her hand. 'The very angels in Heaven can't sing more sweetly than you.'

It was the second time that day Marion's behaviour had surprised her and Alethea regarded her nurse with a mixture of gratitude for the compliment and resentment at the additional coercion.

'We do not want to stray into blasphemy,' Agnes reprimanded her maid. 'But it is true, you have been blessed with a lovely voice, Alethea, one that it would be sinful to withhold from others due to a misguided sense of modesty. Think of the comfort you might bring your father.' Agnes turned and gestured towards the end of the gallery. 'Your brother is going to recite a poem and might even join in with some play-acting,' she said, her voice full of maternal pride.

But Alethea's eye had been caught by Valentine Evans, who was standing in the light of the central window. Mr Evans's face was undergoing a series of astonishing transformations as he recited a speech with tremendous passion. He gesticulated first wildly, then pitifully, then imploringly and finally with apparent elation, falling to the floor and leaping up again.

'Evans is preparing his introduction. I believe it will be most persuasive,' Agnes said with satisfaction.

Alethea and Marion could only agree, though whether it would have the desired effect on Sir Nicholas was another matter.

'Get Fortuna to teach you some dances,' Agnes told her daughter before departing for the kitchen to consult with Tickell. She paused in the doorway to call for Marion to accompany her.

'Shouldn't I stay here with the children?' Marion asked with unusual solicitude.

'They will be fine without you,' Agnes told her.

Marion took a lingering look at the various activities the players were engaged in before reluctantly following her mistress.

Freed from supervision, Alethea wandered down to the far end of the gallery, where Fortuna was dancing a cinquepace with William while one of the players beat time on a drum. Her brother was much better at dancing than she was and she had no desire to insert herself into their fast-paced jig. The prospect of singing to an audience had sent her into a state of great turmoil and she wanted to escape the company of adults before she was made to act in a play too. So, ignoring her mother's instructions, she continued out of the gallery, down a few steps and along a passage she had not explored before.

She hadn't progressed far when she discovered the youngest boy actor, Stephen Wallis, tucked into an alcove, sitting cross-legged on the floor like a tailor.

'Hello,' he said, looking up at her. 'I thought you were your brother for a moment. Are you his twin?'

Alethea shook her head; Stephen was not the first to tell her she looked like William. 'Marion says it is my misfortune not to take after my mother. She believes I must have got my big bones from my wet nurse's milk.'

Agnes was a small, delicate woman with fine, smooth hair of dark gold. Alethea was already tall for a girl of seven years and her limbs were as long and sprawling as a new-born foal's. Her rough hair, the bane of her nurse, was similarly hard to control.

Stephen smiled at her. 'You can learn how to be a lady. At least, I hope to.'

Alethea dropped onto the floor beside him. 'What do you mean?'

'The Evanses are training me up as a player. Mrs Evans believes my face pretty enough for me to play a girl, but Mr Evans doubts he'll make his money back on me and says I'll never amount to being more than a serving-boy.' Stephen looked suddenly downcast.

'But Mr Evans said you had played lots of women on stage.'

'It is his art to magnify in order to impress. I have made some appearances, but not yet to any acclaim.'

Alethea studied Stephen's face. His eyes were fringed with long black lashes and topped with finely arching eyebrows. A small nose sat neatly in the centre of his face and beneath that was a mouth as pert as a rosebud. His teeth were good and his breath did not smell sour. He had long, slender hands, which he made great use of, waving them elegantly in the air to accompany his words. His hair was dun-coloured, but it curled pleasingly over his shoulders in a way that hers refused to.

'I think you will make a fine lady,' she concluded.

'You are too kind.' Stephen inclined his head, waving his hand like a fan before his face and fluttering his eyelashes.

Alethea laughed and copied him.

'Dainty movements,' he corrected her. 'You are not swatting a fly.'

This brought Fortuna into Alethea's mind. She was still somewhat piqued by her father's delight in this small stranger. He had never spoken so fondly to her as he had to Fortuna. 'Is Fortuna the Evanses' only child?' she asked.

Stephen brushed a lock of hair back off his shoulder. 'Fortuna belonged to a troupe of Bohemian tumblers, but they left her with the Evanses when they returned beyond the seas. They said there's no more work for players in England and they did not want to risk imprisonment.'

'Why didn't they take her with them?' Alethea asked, astonished that they would leave such a talented creature behind.

Stephen shrugged. 'Mistress Evans had taken a fancy to her and probably paid dearly for her pet. Fortuna does not truly belong with actors, but Mr Evans says we can use her to draw a crowd, so long as she doesn't distract from the play being performed. That's if we can ever play in public again.' He let out a heavy sigh and picked up a quire of papers. 'I must learn my lines anyhow.'

'Is it difficult?' She shuffled up closer to him, looking at the printed verses with curiosity, though her reading was not very advanced, even for a girl.

'Your assistance will make it easier.' Stephen dropped the unbound pages in her lap. 'You can act as my prompter.'

Alethea stared dubiously at the lines; there were a lot of unfamiliar words. She supposed if she counted them she would know if he'd left one out. She was used to doing that with the notes in the books of music her grandmother read from when she played on the virginals.

'I'll get a beating if I make a mistake,' Stephen added, as if to elicit her sympathy.

'Is Mr Evans very strict?'

Stephen pulled a face. 'No more than any other master I suppose. The others make sport of how slow I am, though Michael invents lines when he forgets the originals and Mr Evans doesn't mind that.'

'You could do likewise,' Alethea suggested.

'Michael is a fine poet; my insertions would only draw ridicule.'

'I am to sing tomorrow.' Alethea tugged at her skirts, which were crumpled beneath her. The thought of having to perform in front of so many strangers, and her father especially, made her hands grow moist, despite the cold draught blowing along the floor.

Stephen, however, was looking encouragingly at her. 'Let's hear you then.'

She felt so at ease in his company, she got to her feet and began to sing a ballad Marion had taught her.

When she had finished, Stephen applauded. 'You made that ditty soar,' he said with admiration.

'But I have never sung in front of so many people. I'm afraid I will squeak like a mouse.'

'No you won't,' Stephen assured her. 'You are a born songster. If you feel afraid just look at me. Sometimes, if I am feeling bashful I pretend the spectators are merely shrubs in a hedgerow. Then I lose all fear of them.'

Alethea liked this idea and thought it would be quite easy to imagine people as bushes. There were some who were prickly like holly, while others were pretty but had sharp tongues, like roses with their thorns. Those who were generous would be hazels and wild plums. Grandmother Ormerod would be an apple tree full of sweet fruit.

'Shall I sing you a carol?' she asked, thinking of her grandmother.

'Please do.' Stephen leant forward, closing his eyes and resting his arms on his knees.

But Alethea had only just begun, when she heard her name being called. 'Will you come with me back to the gallery?' she asked Stephen.

He shook his head. 'I must memorise these first.' He waved the pamphlet at her.

'I haven't helped you at all,' she said, suddenly stricken.

'Your lovely singing has inspired me.' He smiled at her. 'Now the words will float into my head and lodge there.'

She thought he was being very kind and kissed his cheek before running off towards the sound of her name.

'Where have you been?' William was standing in the doorway, looking cross. 'Gregory Alleyn is going to accompany your singing on the lute. They are waiting for you.'

Alleyn was a tall, slender man whose honey-coloured eyes seemed always to glitter with amusement, as if nothing in life should be taken too seriously. A mane of glossy chestnut hair cascaded down his back in loose curls and he shook his head frequently in order to demonstrate that they were his own and not a wig. This action reminded Alethea of a horse bothered by flies, but when she made this observation to William he told her not to be so foolish. As far as William was concerned, Alleyn was the very embodiment of a dramatic hero.

'Ah, so you have netted our song thrush.' Alleyn's rich and sonorous voice carried down the gallery as they came through the doorway. 'At least I hope she proves to be a warbling mavis and not a rasping crow.'

Without Stephen's recent encouragement ringing in her ears, Alethea might have crumbled at this jibe, but now she lifted her head defiantly and went to stand before Alleyn, who was lounging by one of the windows, tuning his lute.

'Lady Agnes has asked for "I Sing of a Maiden"; I take it you know the tune.' Raising his dark eyebrows, he looked down at Alethea with bored irritation.

She nodded and he began to pluck the strings. His playing was much sweeter than his manners and he produced music of such harmonious clarity it was easy for her to pitch her tone correctly. Though her grandmother played the virginals reasonably well, Alethea had never had such a fine accompaniment as this and by the second verse her heart was soaring with the notes.

The rest of the players had gathered round to listen, but Alethea fixed her gaze on the window and, following Stephen's advice, pretended she was standing out in the garden by the shrubbery, singing with only the birds for company. She was startled, therefore, by the sound of clapping when the song finished and turned to find herself facing an audience of smiling, nodding faces.

Fortuna pushed her way to the front to stand beside Alethea. 'You can sing and I will dance. Do you know any *chansons à danser*?' she demanded.

Alethea looked up at Alleyn in confusion and was rewarded with a genial smile.

'Let's see how quick you are to pick up a tune. You can join in on the chorus,' he told her as he re-tuned the lute.

She did not know the song, but the players did and it was easy enough to follow Alleyn's lead. Fortuna leapt and spun in time to the music and Alethea found herself smiling as she was swept up in the joy of singing in unison. But at the last chorus, the players, as if by agreement, fell silent and Alethea discovered she was singing solo again.

It was during the dance that Sir Nicholas entered the gallery. For a second time he was able to watch unobserved; indeed, he was starting to feel a bit like a spy in his own house. As he crossed the floor his progress was arrested by the beautiful voice rising up from their midst. The players were all gathered by the far window and at first he assumed it was Fortuna singing, or perhaps the youngest boy, for it was a child's voice. Something about its purity brought tears to his eyes. He was amazed then, as the players parted, bowing before him, to see his own daughter was the singer. She was concentrating on the lutenist and did not see Sir Nicholas until the song had finished, when she turned round to the sound of his clapping. Confronted with her father, she turned deathly pale and looked as though she might faint. It saddened him that he should provoke such terror in his daughter. He was not a monster.

'Your mother wrote to me that you were proving an adept musician. I thought maternal pride had caused her to exaggerate your talent, but I see in fact she was restrained in her praise,' he said, doing his best to smile kindly at his peculiar child.

Alethea gave a low and rather clumsy curtsey.

'I should like to hear another song. I will stand over here so as not to intimidate you. Choose your favourite.' Sir Nicholas waved a hand at the group before him to set them at their ease, before taking up a position by the next window.

Alethea's heart was fluttering like a bird in a trap, but she took courage from her father's approbation and Alleyn's placid demeanour. She chose a song her grandmother had taught her, 'Ah Silly Soul' by William Byrd. Alleyn didn't know it, but he was able to pick up some of the notes in accompaniment. Afterwards, her father came towards her with his arms extended as if to embrace her, but she inadvertently took a step back and his arms dropped to his sides again. His eyes were wet and she hoped he hadn't taken a cold.

As if to verify this assumption, he coughed before speaking, directing his attention to Valentine Evans. 'You may remain here for another two days, then I expect you to depart. In the meantime, you are the guests of Measham Hall and may enjoy our hospitality as the season dictates. Do nothing to draw attention to yourselves, however. We may have others knocking at our doors and they mustn't suspect that we are keeping a troupe of players.'

'We are indebted to you, Sir Nicholas, for your Christian generosity. You have shown yourself to be a true gentleman worthy of your forebears' illustrious name.' Evans pressed his hands together in front of his heart. 'We will be the epitome of discretion.'

Alethea joined Fortuna in skipping up and down the gallery. She had not been paying attention to her father's words and believed the players were going to stay on indefinitely. If they remained at Measham Hall, it could become an even happier place than Owlcote, she thought.

When she expressed her excitement to William, however, she was disappointed by his response.

'Michael told me that they going to seek their fortunes overseas and will make for Scarborough as soon as they can.'

Alethea said nothing, but decided to ask Stephen for his opinion. He was bound to know more than William did.

→ Chapter Four ←

Christmas Eve

To Roast a Hanch of Venison
If your Venison be seasoned, you must water it, and
stick it with short sprigs of Rosemary: Let your Sauce
be Claret-Wine, a handful of grated Bread, Cinamon,
Ginger, Sugar, a little Vinegar; boyl these up so thick,
as it may only run like batter; it ought to be sharp and
sweet: Dish up your Meat on your Sauce.

(The Compleat Cook)

**Otherwayes to counterfeit Ram, Weather, or any
Mutton for Venison**
Bloody it in sheeps, lambs, or pigs blood, or any good
and new blood, season it as before, and bake it either for
hot or cold. In this fashion you may bake mutton, lamb,
or kid.

(Robert May, The Accomplisht Cook)

'You look beautiful!' Alethea gazed at Stephen in admiration.
He spun round, his silky lavender skirts billowing out
around his legs, before descending in a low curtsey.

Mrs Evans nodded with satisfaction. 'Now I've taken the bodice in, the costume fits perfectly. You'll make an enchanting Perdita.'

'It's a shame we're only doing the last scene,' Stephen said wistfully.

'The audience need to see me dance with William,' Fortuna reminded him. 'We have been practising very hard.' She ran over to William, who was rehearsing a speech with Michael. 'Come, Guillaume, you need a costume also,' she told him imperiously.

William and Michael sauntered over to the corner where the others were standing behind a screen, examining costumes in the light of one of the tall gallery windows.

'Ha, I see you have been given my old frock.' Michael nodded at Stephen. 'The colours are more suited to my complexion.' He stroked his cheek. 'Your skin is too sallow for such delicate hues.'

'Not now that your beard is beginning to grow; the hair is coming in black and your chin is a bristly as a boar's hide,' Stephen shot back.

'Ouch, he wounds.' Staggering backwards, Michael clapped his hands to his heart.

'I can't see any hair on your face,' William said, staring earnestly at Michael.

'Why can't you be sweet like him?' Michael asked Stephen. 'William would make a more pleasing princess, wouldn't you, Will?'

'He cannot be a girl; he is my dancing partner.' Fortuna pulled a pair of breeches out of the chest. They were covered in brightly coloured ribbons from which dangled numerous small bells that jingled as she waved the garment in William's direction. 'You must put these on,' she told him.

'I am not wearing those,' William said, irritated by the little girl's orders. 'I'll look like a Morris dancer.'

'Can I wear them?' Alethea stepped forward eagerly.

'They are for dancing in.' Fortuna pulled a face at her.

'I have a costume for you, my duck.' Smiling kindly at Alethea, Mrs Evans took a plain white shift off the picture hook she had hung it from and shook it out. Seeing Alethea's disappointed expression, she explained that she had a pair of wings that would be attached to Alethea's back.

'You sing so prettily, I thought I would dress you as an angel. I have some gold cloth to drape over you too and a pretty brooch to fix it with.' She began lifting folded garments out of the chest and placing them in a pile.

'When I played Cupid in a pageant I wore nothing except the wings,' Michael told them, as though the lack of clothes was testament to his acting abilities.

'My sister cannot go naked!' William said with great horror.

Michael shrugged. 'Young boys often do.'

'I have an ingenious idea.' Clasping his hands together, Stephen bounced up and down on the balls of his feet. 'William and Alethea, you exchange clothes and we'll see if anyone notices.' He turned to Michael. 'Don't you think they look identical? I'll wager no one will see through the disguise.'

'It isn't Twelfth Night yet,' Mrs Evans pointed out. 'I don't suppose His Lordship will take kindly to such japes.' This speculation was as strong a reproof as the mild-mannered woman ever offered.

'Father is out riding. We could try it, just for an hour, and see who notices,' Alethea said, her enthusiasm outweighing her timidity.

'I'd rather wear that skirt.' William gestured longingly to the crimson velvet skirt embroidered with gold thread that Mrs Evans had thrown over one arm.

'This is Michael's,' Mrs Evans said. 'It'd be much too long for you, my sweet.'

Michael was indeed at least a foot taller than William. 'You'd trip over my skirts,' he told William. 'But your sister is so tall, hers would fit you perfectly.'

William needed no further encouragement than this prompt from Michael, while Alethea was already pulling at the laces of her bodice.

'Here, let me help you.' Stephen came to her assistance.

'Don't go giving the game away,' Michael warned Fortuna as he helped William into Alethea's discarded garments.

'Come on, my minnikin.' Mrs Evans held out her hand to Fortuna. 'We'll leave the young folk to their sport and see how the others are getting on with setting up the scenes.'

Fortuna stuck her tongue out at them as Mrs Evans pulled her away.

William and Alethea decided to test out their new guises on Marion first. She was engaged in painting a tree onto a large piece of canvas and barely gave them a glance.

'What are you doing?' William asked.

'It's the oak tree at Owlcote, the one Lady Agnes embroidered onto the missing bed-curtain.' She stood back to examine her work. 'The players had a spare cloth and said I could add to their scenes. I thought this might bring your mother some pleasure.'

'That's a splendid notion!' William exclaimed.

Marion regarded him with surprise. 'You may add some small details, such as will please your mother, but don't spoil my picture. Here, you can colour in this rabbit; see where I have done the outline?' Marion pointed to a large rabbit at the base of the tree. 'There is some paint ready mixed, but don't use too much.' She gestured to the pot of paint by her foot before turning to Alethea. 'And William, you have a neat hand and some skill at drawing; you may add a bird or some such to the boughs of the tree.' She held a piece of charcoal out to Alethea. 'But first I must find you aprons to protect your clothes. Don't touch the paints until I give you leave.' She hurried off in search of old cloth to pin to their clothes.

'She thinks you're me.' Alethea turned to her brother with delight.

William was not so happy. 'I'll do the drawing; you can paint the rabbit.' He took the charcoal from Alethea's hand. 'It looks more like a pig than a rabbit anyhow, it's much too big, but at least that will make it easy to colour.'

Alethea shrugged. If she got paint on William's clothes, he'd be the one to suffer the consequences. They set to work without waiting for Marion to return. They knew from experience that she had a habit of getting distracted and forgetting the errand she was on. And, indeed, they had almost finished by the time she came hurrying back to tell them they were wanted downstairs. There was no time now to change back into their own clothes and William antagonised Marion further with his hesitancy in descending the stairs.

'Now is not the time to affect ladylike mannerisms,' she chided, as he held up the unfamiliar skirts, cautiously extending each foot so that he could see the steps beneath him.

Alethea, on the other hand, was enjoying the freedom of movement afforded by her brother's breeches and bounded down the stairs, clanking his sword against the bannisters. She was brought up short when she saw the hall below was full of people.

'We have always followed the tradition of burning a yule log in this house and it is one element of Christmas that the puritans cannot object to; indeed, as soon as it is lit the evidence will start to consume itself,' Sir Nicholas was telling the assembled company.

He had summoned the whole household, including the players, into the great hall, where Norris and the kitchen-boy were handing out cups of spiced ale. Beside the fireplace lay part of a tree trunk waiting to be burnt. 'We no longer have the branch from the last yule log to be burnt here, which should rightly be used to light this one.' His eyes alighted on Alethea. 'William, come forward and cut a stick from this trunk to use in its place.'

William was behind her and Alethea froze where she stood. She couldn't possibly explain to her father, in front of all these people, that he had got the wrong child. Spotting Stephen over to the right, she fixed her eyes on his, as though he might rescue her somehow, but he just nodded encouragingly at her. It was all right for him; he had got his everyday clothes on again, she thought. Mrs Evans was standing beside him, a look of consternation temporarily clouding her placid countenance, but then, with a sympathetic smile, she simply shrugged her shoulders as if there was nothing to be done, and her face resumed its benign expression.

'Come along, boy,' Sir Nicholas called impatiently.

There was nothing for it, she would have to play at being William and try not to do anything to make him look foolish. She glanced quickly behind her. William lifted his arms as if to urge her on and so she ran quickly over to their father's side. Sir Nicholas handed her a knife and showed her which branch to cut. This was not too difficult and she managed it without chopping off any of her fingers. Then, with Norris's help, they lifted the log into the fireplace.

'Hold your branch in the embers until it is good and hot, that's right,' Sir Nicholas instructed.

Alethea was filled with pride as a flame from her branch danced along one of the twigs still attached to the log, setting the dried leaves on fire.

'Good lad, give the embers a bit of a stir,' Sir Nicholas said.

She poked at them with her branch and soon the flames were lapping up the side of the yule log. Alethea grinned at William, who was now standing in front of the fireplace. He raised his eyebrows and she couldn't tell from his expression if he was pleased by her achievement or upset that she had taken his place. At least the adults were distracted by the pastry works that had just arrived from the kitchen. They'd soon be absorbed in their conversations and she and William could slip away to get changed.

But then Sir Nicholas called for silence. 'And now it is Alethea's turn to entertain us,' he declared, beckoning to William. 'Her mother tells me she has learnt "I Saw Three Ships", which is one of my favourite carols.' He placed one hand on William's shoulder. 'Alleyn will provide the accompaniment.'

Alleyn, who was leaning against the wall by the parlour door with one foot on a stool, began to tune his lute. Poor William had turned so grey, Alethea feared he might vomit.

'Shall I sing too, Father? I know that carol well,' Alethea was emboldened to ask.

Her mother was staring at her with great alarm; she must surely have seen through their exchange of clothes, unless was she just afraid that William would ruin the tune.

Sir Nicholas was pleased, however, that his son was finally putting himself forward. 'A splendid suggestion, let's hear the pair of you,' he agreed enthusiastically.

Alethea and William stepped closer together, so that they were facing each other and not the room. Alleyn began to play and Alethea launched into the song, her brother following slightly behind, his voice quiet and flat. Lady Agnes had moved beside them so that they were screened off from their father, but now he joined her, slipping an arm around her waist. William's voice quivered, while Alethea's rose so that she was almost shouting.

A murmuring rose up among their audience and it was a few moments before the children realised this had nothing to do with their singing. Norris hurried over to Sir Nicholas and whispered something in their father's ear. The players, meanwhile, were moving aside as a short man, dressed in plain dark clothes and a high crowned hat, strutted into their midst. He was followed by two very tall footmen in equally sombre attire and armed with swords and pistols.

To Alethea's astonishment, her mother seized the tray of small minced pies Tickell had been holding, opened the court cupboard that stood against the wall behind her and, before anyone else noticed, tossed them all in. Alethea hoped there weren't any mice living in the cupboard and that the pies could be rescued, though the pretty crusts with their pastry decorations were bound to have been smashed. But Mother hadn't finished; taking hold of Alethea, she rapidly unbuckled William's sword and belt and threw them into the cupboard on top of the pies. Alethea was afraid she would be bundled in next, but her mother merely gestured to her and William to remain where they were, before turning to face their visitors.

'Master Yeavlea, this is an unexpected pleasure.' Sir Nicholas strode forward. 'You have done well to travel in such inclement weather.'

'Trust in the Lord and He will direct thy path.' Instead of taking Sir Nicholas's extended hand, Mr Yeavlea was staring round the hall at the people collected there. His yellow goggling eyes were set so far apart in his narrow face they were almost on the sides of his head, like a goat, Alethea thought, peeking between the bodies in front of her.

'I had just summoned my household together to drink a pledge to Lord General Cromwell,' Sir Nicholas explained.

'The correct title is now Lord Protector.' Yeavlea frowned. 'For one so recently returned from banishment, you have a very substantial household. Are all these men currently carousing and imbibing potations your servants?'

'I have hired them to repair the house; considerable damage was done and many hands are required to set it right. Of course, with my revenues so depleted and half my land sold off, I cannot afford to keep them all on permanently.'

'But you are here, Sir Nicholas, praise be to God and to our gracious Lord Protector for his mercy. You have seen the error of your ways and chosen to follow the path of the righteous; I would have thought that would be reward enough.' Mr Yeavlea marched around the hall with his hands clasped behind his back. 'They do not look like builders.' He stopped in front of Evans. 'You, sir, dressed up like a popinjay, what is your trade and where do you hail from?'

Evans gave a low bow, flinging his motley cloak back off his shoulders so that only the dark lining was on display. 'I am His Lordship's valet, sir. I was born in Carmarthen in Wales, but my parents moved to Nottinghamshire when I was but a babe in arms, my poor mother sobbing all the way as she cradled my swaddled infant form in her arms, for in her ignorance, bless her, she feared the English and the kind of life she might have among them. My father, a man of strong and noble bearing, though lowly born, was a blacksmith by trade and we lived for many years in a small village by the name of Appleden; I wouldn't expect you to have heard of it, sir, for it was but a humble hamlet comprising of little more than a few cottages.' In several swift gestures, Evans sketched the outline of the buildings in the air before them, ignoring Sir Nicholas's pointed cough. 'I was educated at the grammar school in Nottingham by the learned Mr Littlewit, a man who had received his own education at that illustrious institution, Cambridge University, and was scrupulous in bestowing upon his pupils all the magnificence of his knowledge. Though quick to apply the rod...'

'Precious coals! I did not ask for the history of your life.' Mr Yeavlea's yellow eyes were rolling in his head. 'I would not want such a prattling jackdaw as my valet, indeed I would not. I wish you good fortune with this one, Sir Nicholas.' Shaking his head as if to dislodge the excessive amount of information planted there by Evans, Mr Yeavlea moved on to confront Robert Hart. 'And you, what is your trade?'

Hart's plump, round cheeks rose like balls of yeasted dough and his eyes, despite being half-obscured, shone with amiability, his lips parting in a generous smile. 'I am a stonemason, sir; my previous master, Mr Flee-Fornication-and-Forgive-Our-Sins, a godly gentleman of the most chaste disposition, was fortunate enough to be taken into the bosom of his Maker during a particularly violent bout of sneezing and so I was forced to seek a new position.'

Hart spoke with such sincerity that Yeavlea, after an initial look of puzzlement had crossed his face, did not question this account.

'You don't have the arms of a mason.' Yeavlea squinted at Hart, who was a similar height to himself. 'Let me see your hands.'

Hart pulled off his gloves and held out his hands for inspection. 'The stone has rubbed 'em smooth, sir. I see, by your soft cheek, you used the pumice this morning; well, the stone has had the same effect on my palms, made 'em smooth as a newborn babe's.'

Unable to contest this explanation, Yeavlea surveyed the room again. Alethea, who had been pushed out from behind her mother by William, who was determined not to be spotted, followed the direction of Yeavlea's eyes, hoping they would not alight on her. Alleyn had slipped away, taking his lute with him. She couldn't see Marion either and wondered if her nurse was hiding in fear of Yeavlea's footmen.

Mrs Evans kept her hands pressed firmly down on Fortuna's shoulders and Alethea wasn't sure if she was protecting the girl or preventing her from running to Mr Yeavlea and offering to dance for him. He did not appear to be the sort of gentleman who would approve of such entertainment.

'Is that your child?' he asked Sir Nicholas, pointing at Fortuna, who was twisting and turning under Susanna's grip.

'Win is my child, sir,' Evans said quickly.

'Winnifred?' Yeavlea asked and Fortuna smiled at him plaintively, her dark eyes full of longing.

'Win-the-Fight-For-the-Lord,' Evans announced. 'But we call her Win for short.'

'I see,' said Yeavlea, though his eyes were blinking rapidly as if there were something lodged in them. 'A praiseworthy name, to be sure. I hope she always strives to fulfil her nomenclature. You two.' He waved a hand at Stephen and Michael, who were standing side by side. 'Explain yourselves. But be brief.'

'After you.' Michael curtseyed at Stephen.

'No, no, you are the senior.' Stephen fluttered his lashes and bobbed his head.

'They are my boys,' Hart interrupted. 'I've been training 'em up as labourers.'

Stephen and Michael nodded with great seriousness, adjusting their stances as if, instead of playing ladies, they were now auditioning to be strongmen at a fair.

'Od's bodikins, they don't look as if they could lift a brick between them,' Mr Yeavlea said with disgust.

'I've been mending the sink in the kitchen,' Michael said. 'Would you care to inspect my spout? It stands firm and leaks not.'

"Tis a very fine specimen,' Stephen added. 'Of the smoothest lead. Never drips.'

Mr Yeavlea's look of confusion only increased and his eyes darted about as though he were looking for the nearest means of exit. 'That's a very large log you are burning,' he said abruptly, pointing at the fireplace.

Michael whispered something to Stephen and they tittered.

Mr Yeavlea turned his back on them. 'I hope it is not a yule log, burnt for some pagan superstitions that have no place in a Christian home.'

'Not at all,' Sir Nicholas answered. 'It comes from what little timber has been left after so many of my trees were felled and removed. However many trees I plant, not even my grandchildren will enjoy the splendour of the woods I grew up with at Measham.' There was a bitter edge to his voice.

'All in a good cause, I can assure you. Now that you have seen the falsity of your former allegiance, you must rejoice to know that wood grown on this land has been employed in building up the English fleet in order to protect the Commonwealth from our enemies.' Mr Yeavlea leant into the fireplace, apparently looking for a poker. He gave the log a kick with his boot.

'The fire irons were all taken, along with the rest of my belongings.' Sir Nicholas stood behind him, arms crossed over his chest, looking as though he might kick Mr Yeavlea into the fire.

'Will you partake of a cup of ale, Mr Yeavlea? To drink to the health of our Lord Protector?' Lady Agnes held a goblet out towards him, her voice strained but placatory.

Taking the cup, Mr Yeavlea tapped it appraisingly with one finger. 'Not *everything* was taken, it seems.'

'That is only pewter and was a gift from my parents,' Agnes said quickly. 'If any silver were left us, I would have brought it out in your honour.' She curtseyed, but couldn't bring herself to bestow a smile on their guest.

'May God preserve our gracious Lord Protector and bring peace and plenty to this land.' Mr Yeavlea lifted the goblet to his lips and the rest of the company followed his example.

The ale was rather strong for his taste, so after taking a sip, Yeavlea set the cup down and surveyed the chamber again. 'Are there any other newcomers in the house that I should be introduced to, Sir Nicholas?'

Sir Nicholas also gazed around the hall, taking in everyone assembled there and Alethea thought she saw a look pass between him and Evans, who was shaking his head emphatically.

'We entertain no guests; this is all the household except the kitchen-boy. I can take you through to the kitchen to greet him, if you wish.'

'I would prefer to be shown around the upper storeys of the house. We can ascertain the damage done and perhaps, if it is merited, I might apply for some compensation on your behalf.' Mr Yeavlea was already ascending the stairs and his footmen were close behind him.

'Certainly.' Sir Nicholas joined him. 'I can supply you with lists of our losses that you might pass on to the authorities.'

Evans too was about to accompany the tour, but Mr Yeavlea held up a hand. 'We do not require your presence.' He continued up the stairs and Alethea heard him say, 'Heaven protect me from the wretch's blethering.'

Perhaps it was the male clothing that made her so daring, but Alethea decided to follow them. Yeavlea and her father were busy talking and would not notice her. Besides, Sir Nicholas's heir had the right to roam the house freely. She was in no hurry to put her cumbersome skirts back on and it did not occur to her that William might be desperate to have his own clothes back.

'You must be acquainted with Lord Ingrams since he is a neighbour of yours,' Mr Yeavlea told Sir Nicholas as they entered the long gallery.

'Hardly a neighbour when he lives at least ten miles west of here.'

'His younger son, Benedict Ingrams, is wanted by the Parliamentary authorities for plotting against the Commonwealth. Letters have been intercepted that prove he has been attempting to stir up an insurrection. He narrowly evaded arrest in his father's house and is believed to be hiding out near here before making the journey to France to join Charles Stuart. Anyone found concealing him will face charges of treason.'

'You don't think I would be so foolish as to harbour a traitor? I've made my peace with the Commonwealth and having only just had my property restored to me, don't intend to lose it again.' Sir Nicholas spoke with indignant anger. He disliked duplicity. If Yeavlea was out hunting delinquents he should have made that clear from the outset, instead of all this pretence about a social visit.

'It would be a fool indeed who would risk his neck for a plot that will never come to fruition.' Yeavlea was staring at the defaced portrait with a frown. 'Young Ingrams is a mischievous coxcomb. I met him once – an insolent, conceited creature as well as an enemy to God and religion.'

'I wish only to live in peace with my family. I've seen enough bloodshed between neighbours to last me several lifetimes and would do nothing to incite more.'

'Amen to that,' said Yeavlea fervently.

Alethea waited in the passage while the men talked, their voices growing fainter as they walked to the far end of the gallery, accompanied at a respectful distance by Yeavlea's footmen. It was lucky Mrs Evans had put the costumes back into their trunk, but what about the painted scenes? Tiptoeing into the long room, Alethea hazarded a look. The men had their backs to her and she could not see the canvases anywhere. Perhaps Marion had put them away, though she was not usually so neat.

Hearing footsteps and the rustling of skirts behind her, she turned back to see a figure dart into one of the rooms off the passageway. Thinking it might be Marion and curious as to what her nurse was up to, she left her post in pursuit of the hurrying figure.

The door opened easily, but the room had not been opened up or aired yet and the shutters were still closed over the windows. Alethea glanced around, her eyes adjusting to the darkness. There was very little furniture, just a large press against one wall and a broken stool lying on its side in the middle of the floor. There must have been a lot of dust, though, for she couldn't help sneezing. She was sure she heard a stifled giggle coming from the wardrobe.

'Marion?' she called.

Despite the silence that followed, Alethea could sense the presence of at least one other person in the room. She tried the handle of the press. The door opened a crack before being pulled shut from inside.

Alethea knocked on the door. 'I know you're in there,' she said crossly.

'Shh,' came from the wardrobe. The voice sounded too deep to be Marion's.

There was a banging and shuffling from inside the wardrobe and the wooden press rocked alarmingly. Alethea took a step back as the door opened enough to allow a dishevelled, red-faced Marion to squeeze herself out. Marion's collar was missing and the laces of her bodies were so loose her breasts were spilling out of the top of her smock.

'What are you doing?' Alethea asked in amazement.

'Hiding.' Marion patted her hair, pushing a stray lock back into place. 'From who?'

'From whom. It's a game, didn't they tell you?'

'Didn't who tell me?' Alethea hated to be left out.

'Alethea, Fortuna, some other players I think,' Marion said distractedly.

Alethea grinned, pleased that Marion still mistook her for William. 'You've lost your collar.' She pointed to Marion's chest.

Patting her bosom, Marion's face grew redder. She pulled her smock up to cover her breasts and began to tighten her laces.

'Maybe it's in the wardrobe.' Alethea went to open the door again, but Marion grabbed her by the arm.

'I've a clean one in our chamber. You go downstairs and join your parents in the hall.' Marion stopped, examining Alethea properly for the first time. 'What in Heaven's name are you doing dressed in your brother's clothes?' she exclaimed.

'You're not the only one who can play games,' Alethea retorted.

A snigger escaped from the wardrobe, but before Marion could rebuke her little cousin, they were interrupted by footsteps in the passage outside. Marion ran to the door and seized the handle. The latch rattled, but Marion held fast. Alethea supposed that if she was playing hide-and-seek this was cheating, but, seeing her nurse's determination, said nothing.

'I'll have to find the key for that chamber; it has not yet been opened,' they heard Sir Nicholas say.

'There is no need to open it on my account; I am satisfied with all I have seen.' Yeavlea replied.

Alethea and Marion stood like statues until they could hear four pairs of boots thumping down the wooden stairs.

'They're not playing the game,' Alethea whispered. 'Father's been showing Mr Yeavlea round the house. He's looking for a traitor.'

'Well, they won't find one here,' Marion snapped. 'I don't want Mr Yeavlea to see me without my collar or a kerchief; you know what puritans are like,' she added in a more conciliatory tone.

'They don't like bubbies?'

Marion smiled then. 'Not to look on. Now run along.' She steered Alethea out of the room with a hand on her shoulder, glancing down the passageway as she did so.

Alethea didn't need telling twice. She was surprised Marion hadn't dragged her to her room and forced her back into a frock.

Downstairs, the players had left the hall and her parents were bidding Mr Yeavlea farewell. William was nowhere to be seen.

'Remember, tomorrow is a day like any other.' Yeavlea wagged an admonishing finger at her. 'No one knows for certain on what day our Redeemer was born. The blessed event may have taken place in the middle of summer for all we can tell.' His yellow eyes roved over the hall again, before fixing on Lady Agnes. 'There is no place in England for idolatrous worship, which is not only a great dishonour to Almighty God, but also a malignant breach of the law, a breach that will be punished.' For such a small man he had a very loud voice.

'There is no need to hector my wife. She knows the law,' Sir Nicholas told him irritably.

'Her Ladyship, a born papist, has a reputation for continuing in her popish devotions,' Mr Yeavlea replied undaunted. 'I pray we might become serviceable neighbours and assist each other's households where we can. You will be welcome guests at my mansion place; indeed, I will expect a visit should any news reach you regarding the matter we discussed above.' He raised his sandy eyebrows.

'What is your residence?' Sir Nicholas growled, assuming Yeavlea had taken over the sequestered property of a dead or exiled royalist. 'I do not recall you living in these parts before.'

'Perhaps we did not move in the same circles.' Yeavlea pursed his lips. 'My house, Godstone, was passed down to us through my late wife's family.'

'Your horses are ready for you, sir,' Palmes announced, to everyone's relief. 'We have brought them round to the front of the house.'

'I will call on you again, Sir Nicholas, to see how you do.' Yeavlea bent forward in the semblance of a bow.

The family watched as one as Yeavlea's footmen helped him up onto his horse. It was a very large beast of at least sixteen hands and, perched on top of it, Yeavlea looked smaller than ever.

'Impertinent dandiprat,' Sir Nicholas spat, as soon as the front door had closed. 'Evans, I want a word.' He stormed into the parlour, Valentine Evans following behind.

✦ Chapter Five ✦

Christmas Day

Triumphs and Trophies in Cookery, to be used at Festival Times, as Twelfth Day, &c.

Make the likeness of a Ship in pasteboard, ... place your Ship firm in a great Charger; then make a salt round about it, and stick therein egg-shells full of ... rose-water. Then in another Charger have the proportion of a Stag made of course paste, with a broad arrow in the side of him, and his body filled up with claret wine. In another Charger at the end of the Stag have the proportion of a Castle made of pasteboard, ... At each side of the Charger wherein is the Stag, place a Pie ... in one of which let there be some live Frogs, in the other live Birds; ... being all placed in order upon the Table, before you fire the trains of powder, order it so that some of the Ladies may be perswaded to pluck the Arrow out of the Stag, then will the Claret wine follow as blood running out of a wound. ... fire the train of the Castle ... then fire the trains of one side of the Ship as in a Battle ... the Ladies take the egg shells full of sweet waters and throw them at each other. All dangers being seemed over, ... you may suppose they will desire to see what is in the pies; where lifting first the lid off one pie, out skips some Frogs, which makes the Ladies to skip and shreek; next after the other pie, whence comes out the Birds; who by a natural instinct flying at the light, will put out the candles: so that what with the flying Birds and skipping Frogs, the one above, the other beneath, will cause much delight and pleasure to the whole company.

(Robert May, *The Accomplisht Cook*)

C hristmas morning arrived with another layer of frost. The road to the house and all the trees along it sparkled. Then came clouds and hailstones battering anyone who ventured out with a fury that felt vindictive. The Hawthornes and their servants, glad to be safely indoors, spent much of the morning in prayers led by Sir Nicholas. Knowing it distressed his wife not to be able to attend Mass, he did his best to make up for the lack of a priest. He had said nothing to her about the man Yeavlea was looking for or his conversation with Evans, for fear of upsetting her further.

Sir Nicholas had invited the Thornlys over from the Grange; they were fellow papists and the two families had known each other for generations. He was also indebted to John Thornly for his good husbandry, which had ensured the Hall was well supplied with victuals, and wanted the Thornlys to partake of the meal Tickell was cooking. Yeavlea's visit the previous day had so enraged Sir Nicholas that, instead of becoming more cautious, he had agreed to Tickell's request to prepare a feast worthy of the season.

Old John Thornly had promised that, whatever the weather brought, they would walk over first thing so that they might join the family prayers. Sir Nicholas was surprised, then, when the family failed to appear, but assumed the bad conditions outside had made it too difficult to travel even the short distance from the Grange.

As they knelt in prayer, Alethea could hear the sounds of furniture being moved into the hall and soon the smell of roasting meat and herbs came drifting under the parlour door, making her long for dinner. As if to punish her for thinking of her belly instead of her soul, she was seized with a cramp in her right leg. She grabbed her calf, scrunching up her face in an effort not to cry out.

Seeing her contorted face, William looked over with genuine concern and, after some mimed discourse, showed her how to knead her leg until the pain dissipated. She smiled gratefully at him, glad that he seemed to have forgiven her for disappearing off in his clothes the previous day. After Mr Yeavlea had gone, Alethea had found William in their room in a state of high dudgeon. Mother had given him the worst scolding of his life, he said. She'd threatened to have him beaten for playing such dangerous games. Who knew what Yeavlea might accuse them of if he'd noticed their children were dressed in the clothes of the other sex. He'd probably have them up for witchcraft, Mother had railed. William didn't know what sort of punishment she might finally have sentenced him to if Mrs Evans hadn't come to his rescue and explained that he had been rehearsing a part for their Christmas masque when he was called downstairs and hadn't had time to change his costume.

What made it worse was that by the time Alethea returned, Mother was too busy with their father to castigate her and she got off scot-free. William had been sulking since then and this was his first act of kindness towards her. Alethea considered being racked with the cramp a small price to pay if it won back her brother's favour. Though she often struggled to accept his superior position in the household, she was devoted to William and couldn't bear it when he was angry with her.

As soon as the prayers were over, the children scrambled to their feet and Alethea was close on William's heels as he entered the hall. Forgetting his earlier suffering, William reached for his sister's hand and they jumped up and down with excitement at the transformation that had taken place. Two long tables brought in from the kitchen stood side by side, both heaped with sprigs of greenery garlanded with cherry-red ribbons. Beeswax candles glowed from the middle of holly wreaths placed at intervals down the length of each table.

The whole family watched in delight as platter after platter was carried aloft from the kitchen by a procession of masked servants. Where had they all come from? Alethea marvelled. Each dish was piled high with dainties: from pickled oysters to Bologna sausages, from pies topped with towering crusts of puff-pastry to yolk-yellow custards strewn with coloured comfits. But best of all were the wafers of marzipan decorated with angels whose gold-leaf wings had been brushed on with feathers. Alethea watched their progress eagerly, noting where these were to be set down. At the end of the procession came a little drummer beating time.

William nudged his sister. 'That's Fortuna.'

As he pointed to the drummer, she began beating her little drum double time and the platters were placed on the tables with great solemnity. Drawing themselves up, the servers began to sing, only to be interrupted by the arrival on the stairs of a bearded man in a high crowned hat, who was dressed in a great variety of scarves and garters, all crossed and in different colours.

'Why, gentlemen, would you have kept me out? Christmas, old Captain Christmas?' this extraordinary figure bellowed.

Thrilled and terrified in equal measure, Alethea clung on to William's arm and they watched with open mouths as Captain Christmas continued his dramatic speech.

'Pray you, let me be brought before my master; I'll not be answered else.' The captain bowed to Sir Nicholas, before turning to address the children. 'Did you not wish for me for a merry Christmas?'

Alethea nodded earnestly and William cried, 'Yes, yes we did!'

'And now ye have me.' Captain Christmas smiled at them. 'They would not let me in, you know! I must come another time! A good jest, as if I could come more than once a year! Why, I am no dangerous person, and so I told a certain puritan who came to visit.' Bending his legs, he strutted up and down the stairs and, despite the difference in height, it was as if Mr Yeavlea had returned. Everyone in the hall laughed and the captain shook his head. 'I am old Christmas still, and though I come out of Pope's-head Alley, as good a Protestant as any in my parish.' He lowered his voice slightly so that he seemed to be speaking confidentially to each person standing below him. 'The truth is, I have brought a masque here, of my own making, and do present it by a set of my sons, good dancing boys all.'

Extending his hands, he swept them wide in the air to encompass the new servants and they bowed, one at a time, as he introduced them by name. Misrule wore a short cloak and carried a cheese, Minced Pie was a woman bearing a pie, New-Year's-Gift wore a serving-man's blue coat and had a sprig of rosemary in his hat. Wassail offered up a bowl of beer, while Carol, with a nod to Alethea, put a flute to his lips. Last came Baby-Cake the drummer whom William had recognised as Fortuna.

Sir Nicholas shook his head, but couldn't help joining in with the laughter and applause. 'I know this speech; 'tis from a masque by Ben Jonson,' he told Agnes.

The family were seated at the top of the higher table. Captain Christmas sat at the other end of the table, beside Mrs Evans, and the two of them kept everyone entertained with their boisterous conversation. Once all the food had been served, most of the players joined the household servants at the lower table. Only New-Year's-Gift took his role as serving-man so seriously he remained in character, waiting on Sir Nicholas and Agnes, serving their wine and making sure they had all they desired.

'Can I keep him?' Sir Nicholas asked Christmas, only half in jest.

Christmas chuckled. 'I' faith, poor Palmes has never been much of an actor; perhaps he would perform better as a servant.'

Alethea was surprised to see Misrule take a seat beside Marion and glanced at her father to see if he would object, but he merely nodded in the actor's direction. When Misrule pushed back his velvet cap and several locks of glossy chestnut hair fell out, Alethea recognised Gregory Alleyn beneath the painted face. She watched in disgust as Alleyn fed oysters and anchovies to her nurse, who sat giggling and licking her greasy lips in a most unbecoming fashion. Alleyn might play the lute well, but he was a clumsy server. A slice of duck fell from the point of his knife into Marion's bosom and he slid his fingers beneath her smock to retrieve it.

Marion had become so careless of her attire, Mother was bound to chastise her, Alethea thought, remembering Marion's appearance when she emerged from the wardrobe the previous day. But her mother was distracted by a speech being delivered by Captain Christmas and did not appear to notice Marion's slovenly behaviour.

Alethea was wondering if she could slip over to sit beside Stephen at the other table where the diners were laughing more freely and appeared to be having more fun, when the Thornlys were led into the hall and up to their table by Norris.

'Forgive us for being so tardy,' Thornly said, bowing to Sir Nicholas. 'We found Mr Yeavlea lying unconscious on the side of the road not far from the Hall.' He grasped the shoulder of the handsome young lad standing beside him. 'My son managed to catch his horse, which must have thrown him. Maybe it slipped on the ice; the road is treacherous. We feared at first that the man was dead, for he was half-frozen and not moving, but we lifted him onto his horse and brought him here, it being closer than the Grange. Tickell managed to get some aqua vitae into him, before he lost consciousness again. He's been placed on a bed by the kitchen fire, for to warm him through, though goodness knows if he'll recover.'

Sir Nicholas and his wife looked as if they had been turned to stone, and indeed, Agnes was as white as alabaster.

'We cannot let Yeavlea into the hall,' she whispered.

'You need have no fear on that account, My Lady, the fellow is not well enough to move beyond the kitchen,' Mrs Thornly told her. 'He has a nasty gash on his head, which I have bound up as best I could.'

Sir Nicholas rose to his feet. 'I'll check on the man myself. What was he doing out unaccompanied? You saw no other riders on the road?' he asked Thornly sharply.

'Not a soul.' Thornly shook his head.

Chapter Five

Stirring herself, Agnes also got up to find seats for the Thornlys, casting anxious glances in the direction of the kitchen as she did so.

'Do not be afraid, Mother,' William said, taking Agnes's hand. 'If Yeavlea dares to show his face here, Captain Christmas will soon dispatch him.' He gazed admiringly up at the colourfully attired Christmas.

'Ha, ha, indeed, we will truss him up like a capon,' Christmas cried.

Such actions were proved unnecessary, however, for when Sir Nicholas returned from the kitchen, he confirmed Yeavlea's incapacitated condition, assuring his wife that the man presented no threat to them. Tickell would keep an eye on Yeavlea and make sure he did not venture into any other part of the house. Finishing their feast more rapidly than they might otherwise have done, the family retired upstairs, where the players were to entertain them.

Even Sir Nicholas gasped in amazement as he and his guests stepped into a verdant clearing where leafy boughs arched over them and colourful flowers grew all around. The players had covered the walls with painted canvases transforming the long gallery into a magical garden.

'Look, Mother,' Alethea said. 'Marion, William and I helped to paint this scene.' She led Agnes to one of the newly painted cloths, which was covered in a huge oak tree, its branches full of birds. 'I coloured in this rabbit.' Alethea pointed to one of the rabbits nibbling the grass at the base of the tree.

Lifting her daughter up into her arms, Agnes kissed Alethea's cheeks. 'It is the most beautiful gift I have ever received.' She cast one of her glorious smiles on William and Marion, who were standing next to her. 'How fortunate I am to be surrounded by such love and kindness. Your thoughtfulness is ample compensation for my lost hangings. I shall no longer mourn the originals, but delight in your work instead.'

'It doesn't bear close scrutiny and we hadn't much time to complete it,' Marion said quickly.

'It is a demonstration of your care for me and as such more valuable than the most renowned artist's painting,' Agnes insisted, stroking William's head with her free hand.

'I drew the squirrel,' he told her.

'Why, it is just like the pet squirrel I had as a child,' Agnes exclaimed.

William leant into his mother's side. He felt like a lantern that has just been lit and could almost see a halo of golden light encircle them; his whole being was suffused with such joy to have not only regained his mother's approval, but to have brought her this degree of happiness.

The adults were called to their seats at the other end of the gallery and the children hurried off to find Mrs Evans, who was waiting with their costumes. The performances, a series of acts, songs and dances, were about to begin.

'Am I in Hell?'

Yeavlea opened his eyes to see an inferno of flames blazing before him. His body was being consumed by a terrible heat, while imps were assaulting him, battering his skull from inside his head. His whole body was tortured with pain as if it was being stretched on a rack. He cried out in agony but no one answered his call. Was he alone, the only sinner cast into this scalding-house?

How could this be? All his earthly life he had been convinced that he was one of the elect. His parents and ministers had all seen the signs. His wife had been sure of it. Clasping his hands to his face, he rocked from side to side. He could not spend eternity apart from his beloved wife; that would be a worse torment than any physical suffering.

Forcing himself up onto his elbows, he stared about him in terror. Opposite him, a man was sleeping in a chair. He was an ordinary-looking fellow, without horns or any other such devilish embellishments, but for all Yeavlea knew, a tail, sprouting from his fundament, lay coiled beneath him on his seat. And though the man's snores might seem incompatible with the torments of damnation, he was perhaps the very embodiment of Sloth. Yeavlea had the impression he had seen the man before, probably in the stocks, or drunk outside a tavern. But how could they have ended up in the same place?

Sitting upright, Yeavlea pressed a hand to his head only to find a cloth had been bound round it. There was no sign of his hat, but he supposed there were no hats in Hell. The fire, he saw now, was confined to a large fireplace such as one would find in a kitchen. This would explain the heat, which Yeavlea was unaccustomed to, for he kept few fires lit at home and certainly none blazed like the one before him.

A variety of rich smells were assaulting his nostrils and an unpleasant queasiness stirred in his belly. He placed his feet tentatively on the floor and was glad to find them resting on solid stone. He had half-feared there would be nothing but a great chasm below him into which he would soon plummet. Blinking slowly, he began to take in his surroundings. Copper pots and pans hung on the wall along with bunches of herbs. Shelves were stacked with bottles, jars and various cooking utensils. He shuddered to think of the sort of devilish potions these were used to concoct.

He was surprised then to discover that he had been lying on a truckle bed. In truth it was odd that his head appeared to have been bandaged, but who could account for the sort of tricks the Devil might play? No doubt it amused Satan to toy with mortals in this manner.

Yeavlea's mouth was parched and, seeing a tumbler full of liquid left on a stool by his bed, he raised it to his lips without thinking. The drink was sweet and though the first mouthful burnt his throat, with the second sip he found his stomach settling and his head beginning to clear. It was only then he considered how foolish he had been to sup of this mysterious physick. What would become of him now that he had tasted this poison?

Feeling too weak to induce himself to vomit, he smelt the dregs left in the cup. Perhaps it was some healthful medicine, he consoled himself, for it had revived him. 'You are one of the saved,' he told himself. 'Now you must prove yourself.' He had clearly been the recipient of some angelic aid and must hold that at the forefront of his mind instead of allowing himself to sink into the abomination of despair.

Standing with difficulty, he made his way slowly towards a side door, stopping beside a table for a moment to catch his breath. His ribs hurt terribly and it occurred to him that he might have been attacked. A cloudy memory came to him of riding out that morning; at least he hoped it was that morning. Perhaps he had been set upon by robbers, or even traitors intent upon murdering him. That Ingrams fellow for instance, the one plotting against Parliament.

His eyes alighted on a bottle of cordial. It smelt and tasted like the medicine left by his bed, so he poured himself a cup and, finding it even more efficacious than the first, drank another.

Thus fortified, he left the kitchen and made his way along a passage that opened out onto a grand hall. It was here he caught strains of music. He had never heard such a variety of instruments playing together in harmony before. Indeed, he had never heard any music other than the singing of psalms, although he had on occasion been assaulted by the raucous cacophony that spilt out of alehouses to pollute the ears of passers-by. He stopped again, leaning against the wall for support and as he listened a child's voice began to sing.

All at once, Yeavlea was standing beside his wife on a Sunday while their son sang a psalm. The memory was so strong it was as though the intervening years had melted away and he was back in his parlour in those happy days, long before the wars that killed his sweet boy.

A sense of elation came over Yeavlea. Was he to be reunited with his wife and son at last? His life since their departures had been a bleak wilderness, no matter how he tried to fill it in service of the cause for which his son had died.

He scarcely noticed the tables in the hall with their evergreen decorations as he stumbled forwards, led on by the angelic music. The effort of climbing the stairs forced him to bend almost double and he had to clutch on to the bannisters to haul himself up, but he was determined to ascend to the source of the heavenly singing.

He had nearly accomplished his goal when his foot slipped and he was brought painfully onto his knees, banging his forehead on the step above him. He remained in this position, crouching on the stairs, until his head stopped spinning. Putting out one hand, he felt, before he saw, what it was that had caused his fall. Slippery folds of crimson material cascaded down the stairs like a river of fire. Yeavlea was seized anew with trepidation. Had he been following a siren's call? Was this a test of his faith – one that he had failed? Or should he persevere in his quest? Did those travelling towards Zion not have their difficulties and discouragements on the way? How weak a sinner was he if he should give up now.

Lifting his eyes upwards, Yeavlea almost fell backwards, for, standing over him, with a triumphant grin spread across its childlike face, was an evil spirit the size of a witch's imp. This succubus held the cloth on which he had stumbled between its infant hands and clearly took great delight in having occasioned his fall.

A little drum hung suspended by ribbons from the creature's neck and, dropping the treacherous cloth, it began to beat upon this drum with such force it could only have been summoning its satanic accomplices up from the depths of Hell. The sound stirred up the nausea in Yeavlea's belly and sent torturous pains stabbing through his aching head like so many daggers. He groaned and writhed, tormented by the devilish playing.

All at once the drumming stopped and, daring to look up again, Yeavlea saw the imp had disappeared. He would not allow the Devil to get the better of him. If his wife and son were up there he would find them. He had become entangled in the silken cloth and, instead of attempting to cast it off, he wrapped it around him as a form of protection from whatever he might next encounter.

Crawling onwards with difficulty, he progressed towards the light that glowed through an open doorway. Passing through this doorway, he found himself in a garden. It was no longer winter, nor even night, but a spring morning. A gentle dawn light illuminated a flowery bower and he gazed up into the leaves of an oak tree. His heart filled with joy and he felt all his earthly pains falling away.

In the midst of this clearing, a gentleman was standing before the statue of a woman denouncing his own hard heart, which, he claimed, was stonier even than the marble of the statue. A girl knelt at the statue's feet. Neither of them appeared to notice Yeavlea's presence and, not knowing whether they were angels, devils, or saved souls like himself, he sat down to observe them. It soon became apparent from their conversation that the statue had been made in the image of a much beloved wife and mother and that the widower, a gentleman called Leontes, blamed himself for the death of his lady.

Though Yeavlea hated any form of idolatry, he could not stop the tears pouring from his eyes and his own heart ached in sympathy with the anguish of Leontes. So when an attendant lady, whose name he had gathered was Paulina, offered to cover the statue that was causing such distress, Yeavlea found himself crying out with his fellow widower, 'Do not draw the curtain. Let it be, let it be!'

They all turned, looking at him in startled surprise.

'Which character is he?' a voice called out from the shadows. 'That strange-looking fellow all wrapped in red?'

Leontes crouched down by Yeavlea's elbow. 'My dear sir, you cannot be here,' he said.

'Am I not one of the elect of God?' Yeavlea cried out in desperation. 'Surely I am not to be cast out of Paradise when I have only just gained entry?'

'The poor cove is raving,' Paulina said.

'He's drunk more like,' the daughter observed, rising to her feet and losing all the gracious modesty Yeavlea had just been admiring.

'I am a good sober Christian,' Yeavlea insisted. 'And never touch anything stronger than small beer.'

Raising a restraining hand towards his daughter and Paulina, Leontes bent down over Yeavlea. 'You are indeed one of God's chosen children,' he reassured Yeavlea. 'Come, come, my dear fellow, recline here while choruses of angels serenade you.' Helping Yeavlea move to one side, Leontes propped him up on a pile of cushions. 'Take a sip of ambrosia, 'twill soothe your spirit.'

A cup was pressed to Yeavlea's lips and he drank the perfumed water down in one long gulp, for he had already grown thirsty again. He had never known such unquenchable thirst. The cup was refilled and, sinking back against the cushions, Yeavlea resumed the role of observer, glad that the family had returned to addressing the statue and ignoring him. That was until Paulina, with a stern look, instructed him to leave at once or else be ready for more amazement. She was going to bring the statue to life, but promised she was not assisted by any wicked powers. 'Those that think it is unlawful business I am about, let them depart,' she declared.

Yeavlea could not have stirred even if he had wanted to, for he was utterly transfixed. Besides, Paulina seemed an honest, upright gentlewoman and he could not believe her in league with the cloven-footed foe.

'Proceed,' her master told her, to Yeavlea's great relief. 'No foot shall stir.'

Cheers and clapping echoed round them as Paulina called for music and all at once musicians stepped out of the shadows and began to play. Yeavlea understood now what was meant by music playing upon the heartstrings, for each delicate and exultant note plucked at his very core. He felt as though his heart might burst it was so full of longing and, aye, of love too, love both human and spiritual. This must surely be the music of angels, for devils could not produce sounds of such purity they called forth man's deepest affections.

But more was yet to come, for the statue was beginning to move. Her fingers were twitching and a foot emerged from beneath her flowing robes. Slowly, slowly her slippered foot inched forward, until she was stepping down from her pedestal and moving towards her husband, her hands reaching out for his. The white stone was flaking off her forehead as she wrinkled her brow and her face was revealed to be that of a plain-looking woman, which only made her more lovely to Yeavlea, who set no store by earthly beauty. With a great sigh, the statue threw her arms about her husband's neck.

'O, she's warm!' the former widower exclaimed.

'It is the resurrection!' Yeavlea leapt up, the red cloth unravelling to form a crimson pool about his feet. 'The dead are raised!' He stared wildly about him. 'Where is my wife? Where is my son? Come to me, Grisell, my paragon, my helpmeet, let me enfold you in my arms again. Grief shall be banished from our hearts and we will never more be parted.' Yeavlea staggered across the floor towards the musicians, before falling to his knees. 'Ezekial, my darling boy, show yourself to your unworthy father; the enemies' cannon no longer threaten us and their bullets cannot wound us.' Tears poured so heavily from Yeavlea's eyes that he could barely see, but he recognised something about the lute player and clasped hold of the young man's ankles. 'When I last held you in my arms, your body broken and bloody, I cursed the day I ever led you into battle. Your mother, consumed by mourning, wasted away before my eyes and I, as helpless to heal her as I had been to protect you, felt forsaken by God. But see, I am forgiven. I have been killed and live again. You too will be made whole and we shall be delivered from all fear and torment.'

Yeavlea raised his arms up in celebration, but was disappointed to see that the man before him, far from being his son, was drawing back, a look of dread distorting his comely face.

'I know you,' Yeavlea said in confusion, wondering what that coxcomb could be doing in Heaven. Something stirred in his memory. Wasn't there someone else he had been searching for?

'I have never met you before, sir,' the lutenist said, moving away before Yeavlea could seize hold of his legs again.

'A very passionate speech, but so strangely delivered,' Sir Nicholas observed to his wife. 'Who is that player? He has none of the skill or refined gestures one would expect of an actor.'

'It is Yeavlea,' Agnes whispered back in horror.

'Are you sure?' Sir Nicholas, who had consumed a great deal more claret wine than his wife, leant forward in consternation.

'Allow me to take care of this, sir.' Palmes, who had only performed a minor role in the entertainments, had been serving the Hawthornes. Now he hurried over to Yeavlea.

Yeavlea had sunk back down to the ground, quite overcome. Great sobs rose up from his chest, shaking his whole body as they spilt forth from his mouth. Curling up, he hid his head in his hands. He had never given way to tears before, but now he had begun, he found himself unable to stop.

'Can I be of assistance, sir?' A servant was crouching down beside him, holding out a handkerchief.

Yeavlea pressed the handkerchief to his face. Gradually, he managed to slow the flood of tears, but he was feeling increasingly confused and the pain in his head had returned. This was not how he had been taught the Day of Judgement would come about. Sitting up, he stared around him and was amazed to see a row of people watching him. Were they sitting in judgement? And yet, he did not think this could be Heaven, even if it did resemble the Garden of Eden. In fact, as he studied the shrubbery he began to suspect it was merely painted.

Suddenly everything around him was tilting and all the flowers were whirling around his head like blossoms shaken by a strong wind. Yeavlea groaned. The nausea had returned and he needed a privy.

'I require a closet of ease,' Yeavlea told the servant.

'Of course, sir, pray take my arm.'

Yeavlea was helped to his feet and gratefully allowed the valet to lead him out of the strange garden and down a passageway.

'Well done, William.' Sir Nicholas clapped his son on the back. 'You delivered your speech with great eloquence and your gestures and carriage were spirited and manful.' He did not add how agreeably surprised he had been by William's performance.

Although he had initially opposed it, the entertainment (to which Mr Yeavlea had unwittingly contributed) had put Sir Nicholas in a better humour than he had experienced since his return to England. The afternoon had transported him out of his woes and cares and reminded him of all that life could be at its best. He was grateful to the players for bringing this burst of springtime into their harsh winter.

'Thank you, sir.' William drew himself up, looking as though he had grown a few inches under the warmth of his father's praise. 'I have been practising fencing with Michael, under Alleyn's direction, and he believes I have a natural aptitude,' he said, eager to consolidate his father's approval.

'Alleyn's been teaching you fencing, has he?' Sir Nicholas raised his eyebrows. 'Well, we shall have a few lessons ourselves. I may have been forced to lay my sword aside, but I can instruct you in the theory of the art; it is an essential component of every gentleman's education. And one day I hope you might raise your own sword in the service of His Majesty.' Ignoring Agnes's troubled expression, he put his arm around William's shoulders, whispering conspiratorially. 'I will make myself a wooden sword and we will practise sword fighting, for you cannot learn by theory alone.' Straightening, he said more loudly, partly for the benefit of his wife, 'I must also teach you restraint, for duels are a curse among our hot-headed youth and no way to settle quarrels.' He gave William's shoulder a squeeze. 'Unless of course one's honour is at stake.'

Agnes shook her head, but whatever she might have been about to say was interrupted by the return of Palmes, who, she noted with concern, was without Yeavlea.

'I located a small chamber at the far end of the house where I have left Mr Yeavlea sleeping. It is more secure and out of the way than the kitchen. I hope that is acceptable,' Palmes explained.

'I pray that he recovers,' Agnes said. 'It was not entirely kind to feed him so much aqua vitae.'

'Mr Yeavlea has purged himself quite thoroughly with a good vomit and is now comfortably resting on a bolster,' Palmes informed her.

'It will have done the poor fellow good,' Sir Nicholas remarked cheerfully.

Chapter Five

Alethea was looking about for someone she might talk to and her eye was caught by young John Thornly's. Detaching himself from his parents, who were chatting to Mrs Evans, he came over to her.

'Your singing was that bonny, I've never heard anything so fine afore. My mother said it brought tears to her eyes,' he told her.

'I'm sorry if I made her cry,' Alethea said, delighted nonetheless by the compliment.

Young John chuckled. 'Her tears fall as easily as rain from the sky; Mother will tell thee that herself.'

'Did you really catch Mr Yeavlea's horse?' Alethea asked, remembering the huge animal with awe and wondering how John, who couldn't be more than twelve years of age, had tamed it.

John smiled indulgently at her. 'Weren't so difficult; I'm accustomed to dealing with cart-horses and oxen and suchlike.'

'Did you recognise Marion?' William came over beside Alethea.

'Was she playing the statue?' Alethea asked.

'Yes,' he said with a laugh. 'Alleyn persuaded her to take the part. She was much better than I expected, even with Mr Yeavlea's interruption.'

'I didn't recognise her until the very end, when she spoke.' Alethea still found it hard to believe her cross-patch nurse had performed in a play, even if it was only one scene and Marion had spent most of it standing in silence. 'She looked better covered in white paint,' she noted thoughtfully.

William laughed again. 'That is cruel. Marion is a comely wench, or so Alleyn says.'

Alethea pondered this. She had not intended to be unkind, but she had never deemed Marion in any way attractive and it was quite a revelation that others should consider her so.

'So, what did you think?' Stephen, who had finally changed out of his costume, capered into their midst. 'Did I make a good Perdita?'

'Mr Yeavlea believed you were a girl,' William said. 'And that Michael was a lady; I do believe he was afraid of her.'

'Paulina.' Stephen nodded, his high spirits somewhat dampened. 'Michael played her very well.'

'You were excellent too,' Alethea said loyally.

John nodded in agreement. 'Much better than the mummers that used to come round on Twelfth Night.'

At that moment Marion appeared, her face scrubbed clean. Her skin was now looking more red than white, but her blue eyes were sparkling with unusual brilliance.

'Well, my ducklings, the hour is growing late and it's time you were in bed,' she cried, seizing William and Alethea by the hand.

They looked around for their parents to appeal to, but they were bidding Mr and Mrs Thornly farewell. Stepping back, as though he feared Marion might take charge of him too, young John gave them a little wave. William bowed stiffly in response, but Alethea waved back. John's admiration for her singing had earnt him her friendship.

Marion practically galloped down the passageway and into their bedroom, dragging her unwilling charges behind her. Even young John would have trouble reining Marion back, Alethea thought.

'Remember,' Marion told them. 'If you encounter Mr Yeavlea tomorrow, make no mention of the revels that took place here. And if he asks you about them you are to look at him in wonder, as if he is raving.' She pinched Alethea's cheek. 'Can you do that?'

Alethea's eyes grew wide with pain and Marion chuckled. 'Exactly, look at him like that.' She turned to William, who was prancing round the room, lunging at shadows with his sword, and raised her eyebrows.

'Yes, yes,' he said. 'I understand. We are all actors now.'

'Indeed we are.' Marion spoke more softly and Alethea noticed that a dreamy look had come into her eyes. Marion quickly shook this off, however. 'Calm yourself, William, and put that sword away. When you are in your nightclothes you can come into bed with us and we will say our prayers together.'

Marion's practised fingers rapidly undid Alethea's laces and the children raced to get into their nightgowns, for the fire had not been lit and the room was cold. William and Alethea snuggled in under the bedclothes on either side of their nurse. Marion put her arms around them and hugged them close as she began to recite the Our Father. For all her impatience, she was fond of the children. Alethea fell asleep before she had even finished her prayers, and William, though he fought valiantly to keep his eyes open, was soon fast asleep too, his head resting on his nurse's warm breast.

Chapter Six ⟶

St Stephen's Day

To make an Excellent Jelly
Take three gallons of fair water, boil in it a knuckle of
Veal, and two Calves feet flit in two, with all the fat clear
taken from between the clawes, so let them boil to a very
tender Jelly, keeping it clean scummed, and the edges of
the pot alwaies wiped with a clean cloth, that none of
the scum may boil in, then strain it from the meat, and
let it stand all night, the next morning take away the top
and the bottome, and take to every quart of this Jelly,
half a pint of Sherry Sack, half an ounce of Cinnamon,
and as much Sugar as will season it, six whites of Eggs
very well beaten, mingle all these together, then boil it
half an hour, and let it run through your Jelly Bag.

(Elizabeth Grey, *A True Gentlewoman's Delight*)

The Hawthorne family slept late the next morning, none of
them rising before ten of the clock. Alethea stretched out in
bed, expecting to feel the solidity of her nurse's body, but where
Marion should be there was only a bolster. On the other side of the
bolster, William was still sleeping, his dark hair spread out over his pillow.

She did not bother to wake her brother, but dressed herself as best she could, resisting the temptation to put his clothes on again, and went up to the gallery in search of Stephen.

The long chamber, however, was empty. Perhaps the players were downstairs, she thought, but then noticed that their bags and trunks were also missing. Only the boughs of evergreens and the canvas she and William had helped to paint remained.

Alethea ran downstairs, through the hall, which had been cleared of all remnants of yesterday's feast, and into the kitchen, where she collided with Palmes.

'You are still here,' she cried, throwing her arms around his waist in her elation.

Palmes patted her head. 'Your gracious parents are employing me as their footman. The life of a travelling player is not for me and I have no desire to go abroad.'

Alethea looked up at him expectantly. 'And where are the rest of the troupe?'

'They left at first light. The ice had melted and they feared snow would soon fall so they thought it best to leave while the way was tolerably clear.'

It took Alethea a moment to comprehend what he was telling her and then she had to swallow hard in order not to cry. 'They did not say goodbye.'

'Parting is such sweet sorrow,' Palmes recited, shaking his head. 'It is their way to depart without farewells,' he explained, noticing her tear-filled eyes. 'But Mr Alleyn left you a gift.'

'Gregory Alleyn?' This was unexpected. Alethea would rather it was Stephen who had remembered her.

'Follow me.'

Palmes led her back into the hall. Resting against a cupboard in the corner of the room was Alleyn's lute. A note had been tied around its neck with a peach-coloured ribbon, which Alethea recognised as belonging to Marion. She studied the note. The handwriting was small and sloping.

'Would you like me to read it to you?' Palmes enquired.

'Yes, please.' Alethea took a step back.

'For my little songbird, I leave my lute in your safekeeping and expect to hear you play it on my return. Take good care of it and study hard. I have recommended a music tutor to Sir Nicholas. Your faithful friend, Gregory Alleyn,' Palmes read.

Alethea tentatively stroked the instrument's glossy belly. She had not thought of Alleyn as her friend and his generosity amazed her. She plucked a string and was pleased by the rich, deep hum that issued forth.

'Won't Alleyn need it?' she asked Palmes.

'I expect he intends to buy himself a new one in France,' Palmes said.

Alethea thought Palmes sounded almost disapproving. 'Does Alleyn have enough money?' she asked guiltily, for she had heard the Evanses discussing their lack of funds.

'I expect so.' Palmes rolled his eyes.

There was a noise on the stairs and they both turned to see Mr Yeavlea descending cautiously, one hand on the wooden rail. His skin had a greenish tinge and now, Alethea thought, he looked more like a frog than a goat, since he was walking with bow legs and had none of the sprightliness or enthusiasm of a goat.

'Good morning, sir.' Palmes rushed forward to assist him. 'Sir Nicholas asked me to show you into the parlour.'

'Thank you,' Yeavlea said with a sickly smile.

'Mr Yeavlea.' Sir Nicholas rose from his chair by the fire. 'How do you fare? We feared for your life when you were brought in half-dead yesterday afternoon.'

Yeavlea allowed himself to be seated. The hard back of the chair pushed him upright but he feared the bottom, which had lost all its stuffing, might give way and he perched precariously on the frame lest he should end up on the floor.

'Palmes will bring you a cup of small beer, and perhaps you would like something to eat?' Lady Agnes regarded him sympathetically. 'A little calves-foot jelly perhaps?'

'You are very kind; the beer will suffice.' Yeavlea shuddered slightly, his stomach quivering at the prospect of jelly.

'Young John Thornly recovered your horse. We have kept him in our stables and fed him well. Fortunately he was not harmed, but I am surprised you were riding out alone in such bad weather,' Sir Nicholas said reprovingly.

Yeavlea pressed a hand to his forehead. 'It was not wise,' he conceded.

He did not like to admit it, but he feared he had been subjected to some sort of demonic possession. He had the strangest memories of being conducted into fairyland and fed with ambrosia while elves sang and sprites danced. In truth he had set out that morning determined to catch the Hawthornes and their peculiar household in the act of celebrating Christmas. In particular, he had hoped to unearth Benedict Ingrams, having had reports of a new sighting of the traitor, travelling with a company of players in the Measham parish.

Interrupting his thoughts, Dame Agnes said gently, 'You spoke last night of your son, Ezekial, who died in battle and your wife, Grisell, who departed to God not long afterwards.'

Yeavlea was seized with a paroxysm of fear at what he might have said. Had he been ranting? He was glad Palmes had returned and was handing him a cup of beer. The footman's body shielded his face from view. But when he tried to lift the cup to his mouth he found his hands were trembling so much the tumbler shook visibly.

'Ezekiel was killed at the battle at Preston,' he managed to explain. 'I was fighting there too, under Cromwell. I cannot understand why the bullet lodged in his chest instead of mine. Ezekial was a young man of great promise whereas I...' Yeavlea swallowed. 'Grisell died soon after. I believe grief at the death of our son brought on the sickness that killed her.'

'It is not possible for us poor creatures to comprehend the will of Almighty God, but aren't we who taste of His love so blessed? For aren't our earthly loves but an expression of the greater, divine love?' Agnes said.

Yeavlea was moved by the conviction and tenderness with which she spoke and glad that she did not, as so many others had done, tell him he should be rejoicing that his loved ones had been chosen by the Lord.

'That is the sort of counsel my Grisell would have offered. I must admit I have been lost without her companionship; she was a wise and patient woman. In all our years of marriage, never a cross word passed between us.' Finding a handkerchief in his pocket, he dabbed at his eyes. The fall from his horse, or his brush with Satan, seemed to have affected his senses and made him vulnerable to weeping.

'Many brave and noble men sacrificed their lives in the late wars. I am sure you can be proud of your son.' Sir Nicholas spoke gruffly. 'Though we fought on opposing sides, most of us were fighting for our principles. It was a terrible thing to have to take up arms against my fellow countrymen.' He stared into the fire, watching the flames consume the remains of a log. 'I pray England never knows such violence again.'

'Amen to that,' Yeavlea said. 'The havoc wreaked and the burden on the people has been most injurious. I believe the Lord Protector is our best champion for a reign of peace,' he could not resist adding.

There was a silence broken only by the sound of an instrument being plucked. 'Is that a viol?' Yeavlea asked.

He was sure he had heard a similar note played the previous night. In fact, had he not been serenaded by angelic singing coupled with the most divine consort of musical instruments? It returned to him now, music so harmonious he could not believe it the work of the Devil.

'It is one of the children,' Agnes said, her cheeks flushing red. Rising quickly, she went out into the hall. 'Alethea, what are you doing?' she hissed.

'Look what Alleyn gave me!' Alethea was plucking the upright lute as though it were a harp because it was too big for her to hold on her lap.

'Why on earth did he leave you such an instrument?' Agnes muttered. 'Surely he intended it for William.'

'It was a gift for me.' Alethea showed her mother the note.

Chapter Six

It was only after she had read the note that Agnes registered her daughter's dishevelled appearance. She knelt down to rethread the lacing on Alethea's flapping bodice and fasten her trailing skirts. 'Where is Marion?'

'I don't know. I thought she must be with you, madam.' Alethea belatedly remembered the politeness due to a parent and hoped this might ensure she was allowed to keep the lute.

'I haven't seen her this morning.' Agnes frowned. 'Palmes,' she called to the passing footman, who was swiftly making himself indispensable. 'Have you seen Marion?'

'No, My Lady.' A look of unease passed over Palmes's face. 'Shall I carry the lute upstairs for Mistress Alethea? We wouldn't want Mr Yeavlea to see it,' he said softly, with a glance at the parlour door.

'Please do, and send Marion to me if you encounter her.'

Palmes bowed and Alethea followed him upstairs, unwilling to allow her precious gift out of her sight.

'I have no objection to the playing of musical instruments in the home if they are used to aid the singing of psalms and do not distract the heart from God's message,' Yeavlea was explaining as Agnes returned to the parlour. 'I have never encouraged the destruction of church organs nor the burning of songbooks. Indeed, I prevented my soldiers from plundering churches, though of course we were under orders to demolish all monuments of superstition or idolatry.'

Agnes pinched her lips together, remembering the utter desecration of her parents' local church. The statues and stained-glass windows smashed, the altar rails ripped out and the fonts, vestments and crucifixes carried away by jeering soldiers.

'The lute has long been in our family. The children must have discovered it in some forgotten corner, but it will be put away and not played upon,' Sir Nicholas said.

'I am not here to censure you.' Yeavlea raised his hands. 'I am grateful to you for coming to my assistance.'

'For I was hungry and ye gave me meat, I was thirsty and ye gave me drink, I was a stranger and ye took me in.' Agnes responded by quoting the Bible, partly in defiance and partly to remind herself of the charity due to the season.

Yeavlea smiled at her. 'And the king shall answer, and say unto them, inasmuch as ye have done it unto one of the least of these my brethren, ye have done it to me.' Sighing, he rose to his feet. 'I believe I am fortified enough to make the journey home. My horse is a steady one; it was most unusual for him to throw me.'

'I will ride out part of the way with you,' Sir Nicholas offered, accompanying Yeavlea into the hall. Not only did he want to see Yeavlea safely off his property, he also felt responsible for the man as his guest and, besides, he was sick of being cooped up indoors.

'That is very kind. I hope you will accept my hospitality in return and grace my table with your presence once the weather is improved.' Yeavlea bowed to his hosts. 'The life of a widower is a lonely one and I have no children left to comfort me.' His eyes darted about in alarm at his own indiscretion; he had not meant to confide in the Hawthornes nor to blaspheme against the Lord's great bounty.

But Agnes took his hand. 'We would be honoured,' she assured him.

As soon as Yeavlea had departed, however, she felt weak with relief. It was a miracle he had not seen through the previous night's festivities. She thanked God for sending them Palmes, whose presence that morning had proved so helpful, and went in search of Marion, who in contrast seemed to be neglecting her duties.

After a bracing ride home, Sir Nicholas was in high spirits. Disaster had been prevented, the players had gone and they'd got the better of that puritan busybody. Not only that, but by helping Benedict Ingrams, he had managed to do his sovereign some small service. Ingrams was carrying a memorandum of the aims and objectives of a secret organisation, the Sealed Knot, which he needed to deliver to the exiled privy council in Paris. Ingrams insisted that the Sealed Knot would stir up divisions among Cromwell's followers and help bring about the restoration of the King. Sir Nicholas was sceptical; there had been other plots and none of them had proved successful. Ingrams, or Alleyn as he was calling himself, was no statesman, for all he claimed the Sealed Knot was to be a moderating influence on the more hot-headed young royalists. Sir Nicholas wished him well nonetheless and, now that he was no longer harbouring him, was glad to have assisted the fellow.

When he first returned to England, Sir Nicholas had been shocked by how acquiescent his former comrades were under the new regime. They were subdued, humiliated men who kept their heads down, afraid to draw attention to themselves for fear of arrest or further fines. He'd feared that he had become as abject a wretch as the other defeated men, but this escapade had put fire in his belly. He began to see how he could live in the new England without having to relinquish everything he took pride in.

Despite what he had told Yeavlea, he would make sure Alethea kept the lute – not only that, but she must have music lessons. She might be an odd little girl, but she possessed a talent that should not be neglected. He would find a tutor for William too, and a fencing master. Quite how he would pay for these lessons he had no idea; he might have to sell off more land. Ingrams had mentioned a musician of his acquaintance who was desperate for employment; perhaps he would be willing to teach in exchange for his board and lodging.

Sir Nicholas chuckled to himself when he considered how he had taken Ingrams for an actor until Evans admitted the young spark was in fact Lord Ingrams' son, Benedict, lately returned from overseas and travelling with them incognito. It was no wonder the rest of the players believed he was a minstrel; he certainly suited the part.

When he got home, however, instead of being able to take his ease in front of the parlour fire as he had planned, Sir Nicholas was accosted in the hall by a distressed Agnes.

'Marion has run off with the players,' she cried, her expression a mixture of bewilderment and horror.

Sir Nicholas couldn't help laughing at this. 'Her part as a statue must have turned her head.'

'William found a note from her pinned to the canvas oak tree they painted together.' Agnes thrust a piece of paper at him. 'I cannot believe her capable of such foolishness.'

William and Alethea stood together on the stairs watching their parents and struggling to contain their delight. They were too old now for their parents to impose another nurse on them. Alethea remembered all the scoldings Marion had delivered and thought with satisfaction that she would find Fortuna a much more wayward charge.

The amusement soon left Sir Nicholas's face as he read Marion's note, which she had addressed to Agnes.

'Do you think he really will marry her?' Agnes whispered.

'The rake has no intention of marrying her.' Sir Nicholas wondered if Ingrams was cruel enough to use Marion as a shield from the authorities. No one was looking for a couple; it was a single man they sought.

Agnes studied the note again, unable to fully comprehend its message. 'Acting in a private masque is one thing, but to become an actress...' Agnes shuddered.

'It is different on the Continent. Female actors are accepted there.' Sir Nicholas also lowered his voice. 'The best are well respected. They are not all whores.'

'Even so. What on earth will I tell my parents?'

Sir Nicholas shrugged. 'You can just tell them she found another position; that is not a lie. Perhaps she will write to them herself. I hope Ingrams supports her financially at least.'

'Who?'

'I mean Alleyn,' Sir Nicholas said quickly.

Agnes gave him a wary look, but did not pursue the subject.

Sir Nicholas imagined Marion at the exiled Court. She would fit in rather well there, he thought; he had seen the glint of ambition in her eyes. She might even win the favour of the King, that was if Ingrams took the trouble to introduce her.

'The Evanses are decent people; they won't abandon her,' he assured his wife.

'Susanna Evans is a kind-hearted, motherly woman,' Agnes agreed, dismissing her qualms about Mrs Evans's overly indulgent nature.

'Come, my dear.' Sir Nicholas put an arm around her waist and led her into the parlour. 'You have done all you could for your cousin; you are not to blame if she is a hussy.'

'What's a hussy?' Alethea asked William.

'Perhaps the Hussys are Marion's relatives, on her mother's side,' William speculated.

'Please tell me what Marion's note said.' Alethea looked up at her brother imploringly.

'You'll have to catch me first.'

Laughing, William raced up the stairs, his sister in pursuit. Soon they were running wildly up and down the gallery, enjoying their first moment of freedom.

Acknowledgements

In writing this book I had great fun consulting the following cookbooks:

The Compleat Cook, T.P., J.P., R.C., N.B. and several other approved cooks of London and Westminster (1652, 1694); Grey, Elizabeth, *A True Gentlewoman's Delight ... Very Necessary For All Ladies and Gentlewomen* (W. I. Gent, London, 1653); May, Robert, *The Accomplisht Cook, or The Art and Mystery of Cookery* (London, printed by R.W. for Nath. Brooke, at the Sign of the Angel in Cornhill, 1660); Woolley, Hannah, *The Queen-like Closet* (London, 1670).

Some of the plays referenced are Ben Jonson's *Bartholemew Fair* and *Christmas, His Masque*; William Shakespeare's *The Winter's Tale*.

I would like to thank the brilliant team at Duckworth Books: Matt, Josie, Kathryn, Danny, Rob, Clare, Pete and especially my amazing editor, Daniela Ferrante, for her insights and support. Many thanks also to Rowan Cope for suggesting a Cromwellian Christmas book.

For Colin, with love and gratitude.

Also available

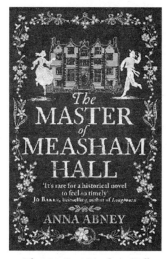

The Master of Measham Hall
(Book I in the Measham Hall series)

1665. It is five years since King Charles II returned from exile, the scars of the English Civil Wars are yet to heal and now the Great Plague engulfs the land.

When Alethea Hawthorne suddenly finds herself cast out on the plague-ridden streets of London, a long road to Derbyshire lies ahead. Militias have closed their boroughs off to outsiders for fear of contamination. A lone woman, Althea must navigate a perilous new world of religious dissenters and charlatans, and a pestilence that afflicts peasants and lords alike.

Page-turning yet exquisitely observed, *The Master of Measham Hall* captures the religious divides at the heart of Restoration England in a timeless story of survival, love and family loyalty.

OUT NOW

Also available

The Messenger of Measham Hall
(Book 2 in the Measham Hall series)

For Nicholas Hawthorne, the Catholic heir to Measham Hall in Derbyshire, subterfuge is part of everyday life. But there are deeper and darker secrets even than his family's outlawed religion: why is his father, Sir William, so reclusive? What became of his mother, and his aunt Alethea? And who fatally betrayed his cousin Matthew?

Nicholas is determined to find out, but as England slides towards invasion by the Protestant forces of Prince William of Orange, he becomes entangled in conspiracies within King James's court — and soon learns that both truth and love come at a high price.

OUT NOW

Also available

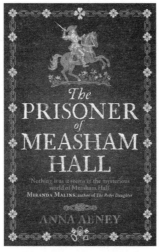

The Prisoner of Measham Hall
(Book 3 in the Measham Hall series)

1690. Sir William Hawthorne, master of Measham Hall, faces a predicament: his loyal steward has died, and he must find another. No easy task given his double life. His problems appear to have been solved with the arrival of the charming Mr Goodwyn. But under Goodwyn's stewardship the world of Measham Hall is turned upside down.

Meanwhile, Sir William's heir, Nicholas, is in Ireland fighting for King James against William of Orange. In order to protect his father from exposure, Nicholas is forced to play a dangerous game as a double agent. When one battle is over, he must return to his home to fight another and defeat an old foe in a new guise or lose Measham Hall forever...

OUT NOW